Open Your Eyes and Soar
Cuban Women Writing Now

Edited by Mary G. Berg

Stories by
Karla Suárez, Anna Lidia Vega Serova,
Adelaida Fernández de Juan, Nancy Alonso, Aida Bahr,
Ena Lucía Portela, Mirta Yáñez, Mylene Fernández Pintado,
Marilyn Bobes, and Sonia Bravo Utrera

Introduction by
Luisa Campuzano

Translations into English by
Mary G. Berg, Pamela Carmell, Dick Cluster,
Sara E. Cooper, Cristina de la Torre, Nancy Festinger
and Anne Fountain

WHITE PINE PRESS · BUFFALO, NEW YORK

WHITE PINE PRESS
P.O. Box 236, Buffalo, New York 14201
wpine@whitepine.org
www.whitepine.org

Publication of this book was made possible, in part,
by with public funds from the
New York State Council on the Arts, a State Agency.

Cover art: Detail from a wall mural on a street in Havana
where artist Salvador Escalones has painted all the buildings over the years.
Photograph by Mary G. Berg.

Printed and bound in the United States of America

ISBN 1-893996-64-6

First Edition

1 3 5 7 9 10 8 6 4 2

Library of Congress Control Number: 2003108945

Contents

To Cuban women of the 21st century

Cuban Women Writers Now

Luisa Campuzano

Cuban literature, unlike the other national literatures of Latin America, was not characterized in the 1970s and '80s by an abundance of fiction written by women. However, in the 1990s, after the collapse of the Soviet Union, while Cuba underwent a drastic economic contraction that had major repercussions in every sphere of life, an explosion of feminine narrative writing occurred that now, as the 21st century begins, has become one of the outstanding features of contemporary Cuban literature. The writers included here are among the most visible and internationally successful of a large number of women writers publishing fiction today, both on the island and in other countries.

In the early '90s, that is, during the crisis referred to as the "special period," as Soviet interest in Cuba waned, the economic unfeasibility of publishing books and magazines encouraged the production of anthologies. Salvador Redonet's 1993 collection of recent stories included many women writers, and Nara Araújo's 1995 widely disseminated analysis of this new wave of women publishing fiction introduced many new voices in Cuban fiction. Although many of those labeled as emerging writers did not continue to publish, and very few women writers who began writing in earlier decades remained active, some are still writing today, and they have been joined by a large number of new voices.

By the mid '90s, the visibility of women writers had changed drastically. Groups of academics, writers, and artists, with or without institutional support, began to organize and put together programs and action plans, convinced of the urgent need to intervene with their various specialized cultural and professional skills in the hazardous contemporaneity of the Cuban woman in order to foment the growth of gender awareness and accord greater prominence to women's history and cultural achievements, thus reinforcing the self esteem so essential in moments of crisis and uncertainty.

The most visible evidence of change occurred with the publication of Marilyn Bobes' collection of short stories, *Alguien tiene que llorar [Someone Has to Cry]*, which won the Casa de las Américas Prize in 1995, in which new topics relating to the feminine condition are described from a very different perspective and employ a new narrative syntax. Another conspicuous demonstration of change was evident in the 1996 publication of the anthology *Estatuas de sal [Statues of Salt]*. A selection of this first anthology of Cuban women writers' stories, edited by the writers Mirta Yañez and Marilyn Bobes, appeared in English in 1998 as *Cubana*. This anthology offered a panoramic view of a long tradition that would provide contemporary women writers with their own legitimate genealogy. It also included an abundant compendium of the literary production of recent decades, without excluding authors who lived and worked off the island, even if they wrote in other languages. Shortly after that, two important magazines dedicated issues to Cuban women and women's cultural production: *Temas* in 1996 and *Unión* in 1997. Young women writers began to win the most prestigious national prizes: Ena Lucía Portela won the UNEAC novel prize in 1997 for her novel *El pájaro: pincel y tinta china [The Bird: Pen and India Ink]*; Adelaida Fernández de Juan garnered the UNEAC short story prize in 1998; and Anna Lidia Vega Serova and Mylene Fernández Pintado received the "David" short story prize in 1997 and 1998, respectively. Since 1999, when Ena Lucía Portela was awarded the "Juan Rulfo" short story prize for *El viejo, el asesino y yo [The Old Man, the Assassin and I]*, and Karla Suárez the "Lengua de Trapo" award for her novel *Silencios*

[*Silences*], this international recognition of Cuban women writers has meant increased publicity, more translations, and more editions of their books. In 2002, Ena Lucía Portela was awarded the prestigious Jaén prize in Spain, for her novel *Cien botellas en la pared* [One Hundred Bottles on the Wall], and Nancy Alonso received the Alba de Céspedes 2002 fiction award for her collection of stories, *Cerrado por reformas* [*Closed for Repairs*] and Mylene Fernández Pintado was the winner of the 2002 Italo Calvino prize for her new novel, *El otro lado del espejo* (*The Other Side of the Mirror*).

Any commentary on a body of work that has appeared so quickly, over such a short time span, requires an effort to establish its relationship with recent Cuban history, to reveal the strategies of its participation (in cultural practice and production) in the complex and dynamic social order of these years, and in the production of transformations (and resistances) that are taking place on the island. Above all, a close reading of these texts necessitates description, albeit brief, of the dimensions of the 1990s crisis, its impact on the female half of the Cuban population, the contradictions between life conditions achieved by women during the revolutionary period, the seeming reversal of these achievements in the early '90s, and the subsequent strategies with which women have risen to this challenge. It is also necessary to recognize the rich development of culture and narrative on the island during the last decade, marked by formal experimentation and the creative appropriation of currents of contemporary thought and art, as well as by the development of more descriptive and polemical criticism. Literary and cultural magazines have played a major role in this dynamic of expansion, as they have become increasingly selective in what they publish and as they have provided greater exposure to new ideas and topics. This has meant that topics such as the textual production of our women writers and analysis of the female condition have been addressed more fully and prominently.

In a general sense, texts by women authors published in the late '90s tend to focus more or less explicitly on the different social and, especially, moral dimensions of the crisis and its repercussions on both the public and private spheres of life. They do not all center their interest on easily placeable referents in daily experiences in the workplace and in family life, both suddenly disrupted by the so-called "special period." Instead, the difficulties of the '90s are approached laterally, with humor and irony, referred to or hinted at in texts that at first sight do not appear to discuss these topics, but on the contrary, often startle their readers with strange characters, spaces and problems that are a by-product of the disruptions of these years. The youngest writers generally omit all reference to explicit social context and to any setting other than the most immediate context (of a person or a group) and they focus on individual voice, on self-understanding and self-exploration that are constantly interrogated and doubted. These are the designated *posnovísimas* and their writing, characterized by its powerful and conspicuous creativity, is inscribed in a transgressive and destabilizing poetics that burst into play in the novels, and story and essay collections from the '90s onward.

Almost all of these recent writers focus on topics previously either ignored or considered taboo: sexualities, eroticism, prostitution, domestic violence, pedophilia, drug addiction. The younger writers tend to populate their fiction with bizarre characters who navigate without clear destinations through closed and often marginal spaces. At the same time, discursive fantasy—in both "pure" and "instrumental" manifestations in stories related to Afro-Cuban religious practices, or in science fiction, as in Gina Picart's *El druida* [The Druid]—reappears in writers who had already established themselves in other approaches, such as in Díaz Llanillo's *Cuentos antes y después del sueño* [Stories Before and After Sleep] and Llana's *Castillos de naipes* [Houses of Cards], and begins to be practiced by others: Bahr's "Tía Enma" and "Soñar," García Calzada's *Historias del otro* [Stories of the Other] and even by some of the *posnovísimas*, such as in Suárez's "The Eye of the Night" and "En esta casa hay un fantasma," and Vega Serova's "Alguien entró volando."

The thematic gamut or panorama presented here is one of the possible cartographies of these recent texts. It first attempts to briefly describe the relationship of these stories to the immediate context in which they were produced. It then goes on to suggest the new paths being opened by these writers' inquiry into the feminine condition at the start of the 21st century, beginning with stories that describe the hard years, the *años duros* of the '90s, which was a particularly severe time of crisis for women since despite all the advances and advantages achieved by women during the preceding years, Cuban society continues to be eminently patriarchal, and this is exacerbated during a time of crisis.

Thus the scarcities, the economic cliff-hanging, and the resurgence—with money sent by relatives abroad, tourism, and the new mixed capital business ventures—of economic differences, and especially moral deterioration and the uncertainties generated by all this, are depicted realistically and emphatically, as in Alonso's "Thou Shalt Not Deviate" and "The Seventh Thunderbolt," or, more often, are discussed from the perspective of a particular narrator, allowing humor and irony to emphasize the paradoxes and contradictions present in a society of official equality, for example in Bahr's "Absences" and "Little Heart;" Fernández de Juan's "Before the Birthday Party" and "Oh Life;" Fernández Pintado's "Mare Atlanticum;" and Vega Serova's "Peter Piper Picked a Peck" and "Russian Food."

Connected with the crisis and described by almost all of the writers either directly or tangentially, explicitly or implicitly, the topic of emigration in all its different dimensions often constitutes a dynamic motif that interconnects texts of varied intentions. Thus, the return of some Cuban inhabitants to their countries of origin, or the eagerness of Cubans to participate in international missions or business meetings in order to travel abroad and escape the penury of the "special period," seen in Vega Serova's "Peter Piper Picked a Peck," Fernández de Juan's "Journey to Pepe," and Fernández Pintado's "Mare Atlanticum," serve to contrast past and present, as well as to wonder about a future that seems very uncertain, and to explore the dimensions of the moral, emotional and identity crises that characters are undergoing.

In these stories by women there is particular emphasis on the description of the conflicts that emigration produces in those who remain behind, whether it is an old woman whose son comes to visit, laden with gifts, as in Vega Serova's "Tan gris como su nombre," or a child traumatized by the departure of his mother, who makes a new life for herself in the North, seen in Vega Serova's "Peter Piper Picked a Peck." In this dynamic contrasting of past and present, deep-rooted family conflicts are exposed and articulated as the scenarios of departure are played out: a sister who decides to stay and a daughter who runs away in order not to leave with her mother (Bahr's "Blanco y negro") or, in a story about a return, new reflections on what the Mariel departures twenty years ago were like and what people were thinking then (Alonso's "Diente por diente").

The topic of raft crossings, the *balseros*, often explored by contemporary male writers, is given a different focus in women's stories, which often describe it from a feminine point of view, as in Alonso's "The Seventh Thunderbolt," which describes the return of someone who has failed in the attempt, or Suárez's "Espuma," where the narrator is unable to deal with an unacceptable death. The presumed clandestine departure of a husband who was molesting his daughter provides a good alibi for a mother determined to protect her child in Bahr's "Olor a limon." On the other hand, descriptions of the mishaps and adventures of Cubans who reach the United States abound as well. Mylene Fernández Pintado has composed an entire group of stories that display both the fascination and the repulsion that the North exercises over the individual and national imaginary, as she deconstructs the popular mythologizing of the "Yuma" (the U.S.A.) in many of her stories.

The reappearance and reconceptualization of prostitution in Cuba can be viewed as a form of emigration that does not always involve crossing national borders, but rather those new borderlines that have been established more recently, designed to protect the tourist business and foreign travelers. In "Anniversary," Karla Suárez explores this topic through the experiences and viewpoint of her narrator-protagonist as she describes her perceptions of these dazzling and deceptive spaces.

Another major topic of feminine narrative in these years is the articulation of what was off limits for decades, for centuries: the taboos and restrictions relating to silenced and concealed bodies. This is linked to reflection, sometimes metatextual, about writing as a space of articulated doubt and self-realization for women. In this sense, many of these texts proffer visibility both to the most violently subtle forms of "private" repression of women, as well as to the writers' strategies of rebellion against this silencing.

Victor Fowler has studied the return to Cuban writing of the '90s of a topic drastically absent in the '70s: homoeroticism, a topic reintroduced most prominently into women's narratives by Ena Lucía Portela, who has made lesbian themes one of her primary subjects of inquiry. It has become a topic featured and discussed by many other authors as well. Incest and sexual violence —long suppressed as topics of women's literature—also became powerful forces in the stories of the 1990s.

Bizarre characters of all sorts, their relationship to others, their social groups and spaces of selective marginality populate Ena Lucía Portela's narratives, sometimes at the service of that perfidiously cultured humor she insinuates into her writing so distinctively and sometimes at the very heart of her text, as in "At the Back of the Cemetery."

As Nara Araújo has said, the topics and conflicts traditionally labeled "feminine" have disappeared from most of these writers' texts, but in those of other young fiction writers, who display other forms and intents, there are thoughtful analyses of the uncertainties, difficulties and struggles inherent in the relationships of couples of all ages, such as in Bahr's "Little Heart," Fernández Pintado's "The Anteater," Suárez's "The Eye of the Night" and many others.

Another theme that emerges in the texts by these authors, often as part of the setting, is the act of writing itself and reflection about what it means to be a writer and inhabit a writer's world. This is an important issue for women writers, as they have come to occupy this space of risk and freedom, of intimate exploration and personal self-fulfillment, of formal search and public projection, of the acceptance or rejection by established authorities and patrons, as in Bobes' "¿Te gusta Peter Handke?" and Fernández de Juan's "Bumerang." This is also a context in which to recall the unique 1995 book by Margarita Mateo, *Ella escribía poscrítica [She Wrote Post-criticism]* in which essay and fiction blend to take charge and exorcize, from various cultural manifestations and the analysis of contemporary poetics and thought, not only the demons of hazardous contemporaneity in which these textualities and topics are produced or discussed, but the life setting within which and about which the author writes, omnipresent in her various personae.

Finally, many novels by women have appeared since the mid-'90s, half of which (many with traditional historical settings) have been by long-standing writers, like Mary Cruz (*Colombo de Terrarrubra*, 1994; *Niña Tula*, 1998; *El que llora sangre [He Who Weeps Blood]*, 2001, *Tula* 2001) and Marta Rojas (*El columpio de Rey Spencer [King Spencer's Swing]*, 1996; *Santa Lujuria*, 1998). Another journalist, Mercedes Santos with *El monte de Venus [The Mount of Venus]* (2001), which stirred up mixed reactions in critics, has featured the topic of homoeroticism that was the subject of prominent literary expression in the '20s and '30s. Among the women publishing first novels, many have prior experience in writing for the media. Margarita Sánchez-Gallinal, in *Gloria Isla* (2001) reflects on issues in national history in the context of a family's history. In *Minimal son* (1995), Ana Luz García Calzada scrutinizes family relationships and conflicts in a more specifically contemporary space, in an experimentalistic narrative based on subversive poetic strategies. Karla Suárez and, especially, Ena Lucía Portela bring some of the most important new voices to the genre of the Cuban novel. In *Silencios [Silences]* (1999) Suárez recounts, extraordinarily effectively yet at the same time with great economy of means, as the title suggests, the coming of age of a young woman during the last third of the 20th century. The events of her life are related within the context of her family and closest friends' conflicts with the society and the history that have affected them profoundly and have demanded so much of them. The most internationally renowned of the contemporary Cuban women novelists, Ena Lucía Portela, in *El pájaro: pincel y tinta china* (1998) and *La sombra del caminante [The Traveler's Shadow]* (2001) is recognized for her major—and extraordinarily effective—innovations in her fiction, surely the most condensed, ambitious and impressive body of work of this decade. Her characters intersect and move in and out, characters who for the most part belong to a small intellectual world, subterranean and sordid, in which social interactions are presented cynically and intensely, interspliced with jokes and humor that pardon no one. Her third novel, *Cien botellas en la pared* (2002), has won an important Spanish literary prize, and will be published in Havana in 2003, as will Anna Lidia Vega Serova's first novel, *Noche de ronda [Night Watch]*, which appeared in Spain in 2002.

There is much more to say. There are all the Cuban women writers who live and publish in other countries: those who have been there for decades and others who have moved recently, those who have done all their writing there and others who already had established careers in Cuba. And there is much more to be said about the complex interrelationships between those who live on and off the island. There is more to say, too, about the body of criticism about contemporary Cuban women writers that is growing daily. Current critics, especially those outside Cuba, discuss the work of Cuban women writers seriously and at length, though they can also be frivolous and superficial when they seek lighthearted entertainment. In this short introduction I have attempted to briefly characterize some of the recurrent themes and preoccupations in recent fiction by contemporary Cuban women writers as they write—primarily with Cuban readers in mind—about current social realities, recent transformations and upheavals, and the different human responses to these changing times.

Translated by Mary G. Berg.

Open Your Eyes and Soar

The Eye of the Night

Karla Suárez

For Ode and Alfredo, for the idea

Because everything has a beginning, and we almost always want to know what it is. It's an insistent need to define the causes that precede effects, and since the causes aren't always clear or perhaps we don't want to see them clearly, then we go ahead and invent them, add details, assign them one name or another, label them with dates and wrap it all into a complete package, so we can say: that's how it all began.

It all began the day Jorge came home with a telescope. I've always been nocturnal. I like wandering around the house in the dark, reaching out my fingers to touch the furniture until I learn it all by heart. Jorge doesn't like this, but I've always been this way. He likes to fall asleep feeling my body next to his. I go along with this to please him, and I stretch out alongside him after we make love, staring up at the ceiling and waiting until he's fallen asleep before I get up. Night fascinates me, I don't know why he doesn't understand this.

That day he showed up at home with a telescope, he said that a friend had given it to him and that I could have fun counting stars. I liked that idea. From then on, before I went to sleep, I'd sit out on the balcony to gaze at the stars, just as he'd said. Jorge would come over, have a look through it, say something, and then a little later he'd invite me to "Come to bed." "Come to bed" meant "Come make love," and he'd start stripping off his clothes and get into bed naked, calling out that he was sorry he'd ever brought home that instrument since I wasn't an astrologer nor was I going to discover a new comet, and if it was stars I wanted to see, he'd help me on that. That's the way Jorge is.

So my late nights changed a bit, I didn't just wander around and peer down into the street. With the telescope I could look at the constellations, I could spy on my neighborhood beyond my usual range of view. My balcony looks over an avenue that rarely has any late night traffic. Beyond that, there are houses and buildings, a park full of broken streetlights, little alleyways that get lost in the trees. I could see all of this. I turned into the busybody of the neighborhood, the eye of the night, and it was odd to think that at this very moment someone could be watching me through another telescope. We are never alone. Darkness is an accomplice with many faces.

One of those nights while I was running my eyes over those buildings, I saw him leaning on his balcony rail. A young man, smoking slowly and gazing down at the avenue as though he weren't seeing a thing, like someone who is just finishing his cigarette before he goes to bed. I'd never seen him before, so I peered at him with interest. Maybe he had the same crazy habit I did, or maybe he'd just had a bad day and couldn't get to sleep, how do I know, the eye of the night has its limits. In this case, he tossed his cigarette butt down and stayed there leaning on the railing. I kept watching him. He and I might be the only witnesses of the night; it's a good feeling to have company in an enterprise even if that venture seems totally absurd. The man lit another cigarette. At the back of his balcony there was a door, and a window with the curtains open, the room dark behind it. I couldn't make out whether there was someone inside snoring like Jorge over on this side, and it really didn't make much difference. The man stayed there leaning on the rail for a long time, he smoked three cigarettes and, as he was tossing the last butt, he stood up, stretched his body and went into the room. Pretty boring, I thought, so I forgot all about the neighbors and stayed there watching the stars until dawn made it impossible.

The next night everything went as usual. Jorge sweating on top of me and me pumping faster and faster to hurry him along. Then the pause. A final sigh and Jorge stretched out beside me face down murmuring a faint "See you tomorrow." Then it was my time, when I could get up, look at Jorge breathing peacefully, and go out on the balcony. The neighborhood as usual, all quiet. Me spying behind my glass eye, like Corrieri in *Memories of Underdevelopment*. It's odd how you start staring at something and your head fills with all kinds of images, if I could just tape record everything that goes through my mind late at night, I'd write a novel, or a sociology book, or maybe, I don't know, you start thinking about so many things... I thought about the insomniac I'd seen the night before, his balcony was dark, he was probably sleeping like everyone else, like Jorge, who is sleeping peacefully in my bed. And why in my bed? Because that's how it is, it's been like that for a while now. First we went out occasionally, we'd see each other, he'd stay over once in a while, then more and more often, he'd leave a pair of pants here one day, a shirt another day, and somehow the house filled up with Jorge who sleeps while I think about things as I gaze at the windows over there on the other side.

At some point, I saw a light switch on in one of the windows. That was an event in these late night hours, and I had my eye focused on the apartment of the man I'd seen the night before. The window curtains were still open. If you've got something to hide, you take care to close your curtains, but he didn't suspect that I was here. He came in followed by a woman, a thin woman with long hair who smiled all the time. A man and a woman in an intimate setting clearly visible to anyone who wanted to watch. If Jorge woke up he was going to accuse me of being a pervert, or he might grab the telescope away from me, you never know what crosses someone else's mind. The idea of keeping my eye on them really appealed to me, and I watched as the skinny woman undressed while he drank from a bottle he held in his hand. I've never seen a pornographic movie, so I was really intrigued by this show. She got into bed and out of my sight; he took off his shirt, lit a small lamp, and turned off the light. Off limits to snoops. The apartment turned into a very dim glow where surely a man and a woman were making love just like Jorge and me before Jorge went to sleep. Quite a while went by and I saw my neighbor get up, take another drink from the bottle, put on his shorts and come out on the balcony to smoke. Exactly like the night before, looking at the emptiness of the streets. The woman must be sleeping and he was as wide awake as I was. He smoked for a while, tossed the butt, and then lit up another cigarette, looking out over the streets just as I did in those early hours. I always wonder what other people think about when they are sitting quietly, smoking by themselves. Jorge never does things like that, we're together at night, only at night. We talk a bit, he tells me stuff, he says he's tired and bored, I listen to him. You couldn't exactly say we're in love, we're not really living together, the clothes he leaves over at my house don't at all mean that we live together. But we're here most nights, making love until he turns his back on me and falls asleep—why do we always say "making love"? There are other ways to say it, of course, but I don't much like them. Would I be making love with the man across the street? How do I know. The man smoked a few cigarettes and went to bed, turned off the light and nothing else happened all night.

A week later I was more than convinced that the man across the street suffered from insomnia and that besides, he couldn't be making love, because you can't be in love with a different woman every night. His routine was a closed circle, a woman, the little bedroom light and a short while later out smoking on the balcony, like every other late night. It never varied, cigarette after cigarette that he tossed into the street while the woman slept on, like Jorge. I thought it might be interesting to go over to his house in the morning and invite him to spend the night with me. I could even show him my telescope and maybe we'd discover something. A silly idea of course, because if you choose to be out there late at night leaning on the balcony rail, it's because you want to be alone and you don't want to be confronted with evidence that someone has been spying on you. But that man puzzled me. Why that insistence on smoking and smoking silently, looking down over the street as if the street could applaud his conquests, his tired face and his lack of sleep? I don't know, men just don't cope well with being alone. He filled up his nights with women, and then what? What's the cure for a fascination with the void? You lean on the balcony rail and that's when suddenly all the truths slip out from behind their masks. Night is the great mirror. You can make a big effort to patch together the big picture with scraps, like parts of an infinite mosaic, but something happens when those subterfuges turn into buffoons making fun of us. What was Jorge doing in my bed? Besides sleeping, turning his back on me, and falling asleep after we'd sweated without loving each other, because Jorge is asleep in my bed and snoring and before he goes off to work we'll have breakfast together and then he'll come back and it's night again, another night when there I'll be, gazing through the crystal eye watching how the guy across the street smokes, makes love and smokes, leans on the balcony rail and runs his hand over his face, tosses the butt into the street or rests it on the balcony rail and peers out to see if anything is going on, like I do, hoping every night that something different will happen, something different that won't be Jorge sleeping on his stomach like the women in the apartment across the way, and isn't it all the same thing? The neighbor at least changes his expression, and who knows if on one of these nights...

I began to feel obsessed. I'd slip away from Jorge's side a little sooner every night to go out on the balcony. He began to get annoyed asking what on earth I was doing in the middle of the night and complaining when I'd find some excuse to not make love. We women have some terrific excuses. Finally he'd fall asleep and I could settle myself behind the eye of the night to wait for the lamp in the apartment across the way to light up.

One night the miracle happened. My neighbor switched on the light, followed by a new woman. She came in, tossed her purse down and walked around the room looking at everything, making comments that didn't reach my ears. He went over to the bed, turned on the little lamp, and went over to switch off the main light, just as—in the very same moment—the woman turned toward the balcony. My neighbor followed her and they both leaned on the balcony railing and chatted. It was strange, that woman kept laughing and talking, he kept watching her and smiling. I assumed he must be tired of so many words and wanting, like every other night, to get to bed to then leave her sleeping and head for the balcony, but he didn't act impatient. He certainly didn't seem annoyed or detached like I'd been a few hours before, when Jorge was trying to kiss me. The man didn't seem irritated, he kept smoking and listening to the woman, who kept smiling and then once in a while would look serious, sigh, and then start talking again. What could they be talking about? I don't know; my telescope is only a magic eye, and seeing is not like being there. All I could really conclude is that I felt really uncomfortable seeing them there talking for hours and hours, while this here-every-night man was sleeping in my bed, and once in a while he'd cough and then I'd be aware of his presence. Yes, because if Jorge didn't make a sound the entire night, then I could swear I was definitely alone, but Jorge always snored and coughed. Physically I was not alone. Physically there were two bodies in my apartment, each one occupying its space, spaces that were connected only in the interval between Jorge's "Let's go to bed now" and when he fell asleep. What was he doing there every night while I was peering into the apartments across the street in the middle of the night? Peering into the apartment where the man and the woman kept on talking. Every once in a while he'd say something and run his hand over her face, smoothing her hair out of the way. He seemed like an entirely different neighbor, but it was the same man, my telescope knew him perfectly well. They kept talking. I was the spy. The telltale eye that keeps watch on plotters who are conferring in low voices, checking each other out to make sure, just a conqueror, taking over territories rightfully theirs. In the hundreds of minutes that make up the hours before the cocks crow—roosters crow a lot before dawn breaks. Jorge wouldn't know about that because he isn't an insomniac. She straightened up, he said something and they walked toward the apartment. They stayed inside for a few minutes, someone turned off the little bedside lamp and he appeared in the doorway again but looking different. He didn't come out and lean on the rail and smoke and look out over the street he must know by heart by now. He leaned against the door frame, gazing into the apartment, toward where I know the bed must be. I'd have liked to do the same thing. I'd have liked to give up my post, stretch my back out and gaze inside, but it wouldn't make sense. Inside, I was only going to find Jorge, lying on his stomach on one side of my bed, still hours away from waking up and wanting his breakfast. So I preferred to just stay on there to see how he stopped gazing at her and sat down on the balcony floor, across from me, leaning his head back against the wall and smiling, without smoking, without doing any of the things he and I are so used to. He stayed there like that for a bit until the woman appeared in the doorway, barefoot, with her hair loose and a sweater wrapped around her. She walked toward the man, crouched down by him and they looked at each other for a long time, I know that. It doesn't matter that her back blocked my view. Nor does it matter that I couldn't see their faces when she sat down holding out her arms and the man's hands appeared on her hair. It no longer mattered to me to see, my telescopic eye didn't matter, nor my lack of headphones that would let me overhear what perhaps they weren't going to say. He pulled her close to him and I knew they were kissing without it mattering that I was gazing at them from over here. Who was I? What effect could I have? Nothing, absolutely nothing, conclusively nothing. I was the spectator who dries her tears timidly while the projectionist rewinds the film. I wasn't anything, that's why they were kissing. He held her very close and they stayed that way, together and happy, and I felt so happy, I was surprised at my happiness watching them. She leaning against him and I seeing their faces, smiling, he kissing her ear while the woman stretched up and turned her face to kiss him and they stayed that way, so quietly, whispering things to each other, waiting for the dawn, to greet the dawn together while Jorge slept on. Jorge's such an idiot; he's incapable of experiencing the birth of a day; he never understands anything. And I stayed there for the birth, I was there when the sky began to flood with light and the sparrows left their nests and they got up from the floor. He stretched his body and put his hands on the balcony rail to shout out something to the day that was beginning while she watched him tenderly, leaning against the wall. Then they embraced again, he put his arm around her back and they went inside again, they were lost in the shadows, they closed the curtains, pulling away from me, from my crystal eye filled with the morning light, without the dim bedside lamp. I stayed on the balcony surprised by the dawn, without accomplice stars in my eagerness to profane others' spaces, without the man and the woman, who must be lying in bed, either making love or sleeping, how do I know, sleeping probably, what does it matter, but he didn't get up again, he didn't come back to the balcony to smoke the way he did at the end of each late night. He left me alone waiting for him to appear. He left me alone the way I am. Alone. A few moments alone and now I don't need the eye of the night in order to make out the cars that are beginning to move along the street, the old men bringing their dogs out to pee, alarm clocks going off, radios blaring the morning news and Jorge rolling over in bed.

When Jorge got up, I was still outside.

"Hey, you should look for a job as a night guard, it would be perfect for you, you're so crazy... How about fixing breakfast now, come on..."

He went into the bathroom and I stayed on the balcony. A little later he came out with his pants on and the towel hanging over his shoulder.

"What are you doing still here? Hey, girl, obviously you don't have to get to work early. Breakfast ready?"

I leaned on the doorframe and watched him while he put on his shoes.

"Leave, Jorge."

He kept on tying his shoes.

"Of course, I'm going to work, come on, fix breakfast, hurry up now, then you can lie down and get some sleep, you've got circles under your eyes..."

"No, Jorge, leave, I want you to leave."

He looked up unwillingly.

"What's wrong, girl?"

"I want you to leave...to pack up everything and not come back...to leave."

Jorge straightened up and looked at me with a slight smile.

"What's wrong? The stars going to your head, or what?"

I didn't say anything, he sighed, stood up and walked toward me with his arms open.

"Hey now, what's wrong with my astrologer? Are you really tired?"

I stepped away from his body.

"I'm tired of you and, besides, I'm not an astrologer."

He stopped and stared at me, annoyed.

"What's going on, girl? Are you saying this seriously?"

"Yes, I want you to leave, to pack up all your stuff and leave me alone, Jorge, leave."

"But why?"

He started to get impatient, but in contrast, I was as calm as the dawn. I sat down on the bed while he stood there, half dressed.

"Give me one reason, Jorge, give me one single reason why you and I are together."

He raised his head to stare at the walls, his mouth twisted, and he took a few quick steps over to pick up his shirt.

"Look, girl, it's seven in the morning and you're giving me this. I'm going to work, let's talk later, okay?"

I shook my head no, and I saw his face harden as he raised his voice.

"You really want me to leave?"

"Give me one reason why you shouldn't."

Jorge stood there for a few seconds looking at me with hatred, then his face slowly relaxed, without looking at me, lost in who knows what inside his head. "I don't know... A reason? I don't know."

"Then leave."

I stood up and went back to the balcony doorway to watch the morning that was beginning to fill with people. I could feel his cold eyes piercing my back.

"Then what the fuck," he started to move around quickly and opened the closet, "I've been kicked out of better places, but when I leave, I leave for good, you hear that?"

I didn't have to answer, there was no need to. I kept standing there with my back to him, watching how the curtains of the apartment across the way were still pulled closed while on this side, Jorge was muttering, and I didn't need to look at him. I knew perfectly well that he was tossing his clothes into the suitcase, was looking for something in the bathroom. Then he came back and pulled the zipper closed, furiously.

"Did you hear me? That's why you're so messed up. No one can put up with a woman who prowls around awake all night. Night was made for sleeping and fucking. You hear that? Go on like this and you'll be even more messed up than you are. That's why I'm getting the hell out of here."

I turned my back on my neighbor's balcony and looked at Jorge with the suitcase in his hand.

"You left this," I pointed to the telescope. "It's yours."

"Keep it. What would I want that shit for? I'm out of here."

Jorge left the room, slamming the door like in *The Dollhouse*. He didn't want to take the telescope, he thought he didn't need it, and maybe he was right, he certainly didn't need it, but I didn't either. I didn't need it any longer. On the following nights, the curtains of the apartment across the way were never again left open. I could see that the light was being turned on and off, but I didn't need my crystal eye to see that. I'd stand out on the balcony awhile to gaze at the streets, the park full of trees, the avenue empty of traffic, knowing that over on the other side a light would be turned on and then later turned off, all through the night, even if I weren't keeping watch any longer, even if I weren't on my balcony to notice everything. I knew that. I knew perfectly well that my neighbor wouldn't be coming out to smoke and then toss the butts into the street. I didn't need him any longer, so I could close my eyes and smile and sleep, while out on the balcony, the eye of the night remained alone, spying on the birth of the dawn.

Translated by Mary G. Berg.

Anniversary

Karla Suárez

Yes, it's me, here, calling from my room, sipping a vodka martini, my favorite drink...how's everything going for me? Honey, it's just great, this city is terrific and from up here I can see the whole panorama..., no, Fabian isn't here, he left early to do something, I stayed here watching videos, lounging in bed with the remote in my hand...of course, he couldn't go, hon, they didn't let the foreign press in, but it doesn't matter, he's done almost everything he wanted to do...oh let me tell you, girl, when we got here we came to the hotel, a five star hotel, hon, can you imagine? with a giant bed my whole family could fit into easily, the room's full of mirrors, it has a huge television screen I don't know how many inches wide and I keep the remote in my hand, surfing channels, music, ads, movies in English, we see all the news broadcasts because Fabian watches them all, but anyway, they don't last long...this is the life, girl, and the bathroom, you'd just die if you could see the bathroom, I have to tell you, the first day we were here I spent an entire hour in there, I took my Walkman in there with me, my vodka martini and my Camels, yes, because he smokes Camels, let me see if I can bring you a pack so you can have a break from those nasty Populares...yes, of course, I smoke them too, but I'm living it up now, once in a while you have to get away from the national brands, right?...where was I? oh, the bath, the bathroom's lined with mirrors, too, everything so clean and perfumed you want to stay here forever, not like at home, with that dinky little bathroom, this bathtub has sliding doors and it's one of those you can stretch out in full length and even swim in it, and you don't even slip because, just imagine, it has little hand things on the sides you can hold onto, no, even getting out of it is easy, hon, and the water is cold, warm, hot, whatever you want, with a little hand-held shower like a telephone, I filled the tub with water that was so hot that I almost burned myself when I stepped in, but even so, I stayed in, if paradise burns, then I want to be Joan of Arc, don't you see, when I get home there's the hassle of heating the water on the stove and then splashing it on with the dipper, what the heck, hon, gotta enjoy this...jealous?...but that's not everything, they put little packets in the bathrooms, you know, like hotels do, with body lotion, gel shampoo, shaving cream and even toothpaste, besides that, there's a roll of toilet paper in the holder and another new one for in case you run out, of course I put the toothpaste away to take home with me, and I'll take the toilet paper when we're checking out of the room, my mom is going to be so happy with the gift because there isn't even any newspaper there...no, girl, I can't get hold of one for you, what do you think, that I'm going to break into another room in order to grab another roll of paper, and now I'll tell you the best part, when I got out of the shower I wrapped myself in an immense towel, just like in the movies, and started to dry my hair with the hairdryer in the bathroom, what a luxury, hon, all that warm air, your hair comes out looking great, all the mirrors cloud over with steam and I was sweating with my ears all hot so when I left the bathroom I had to turn up the room's air conditioning and I threw myself on the bed naked to watch music videos and drink a beer, ah! because there's a little refrigerator right in the room, you can help yourself to whatever you want, this is some life...no, no, he wasn't here, he spends all day at his work and stuff and I don't even want to leave the room though the hotel has everything, listen, everything imag-

inable for us..., don't joke, you know I don't take up with just anyone, I'm no *jinetera*, this is just something that happened, I've
known him ever since the first year, when he came over to the university to check out how we study journalism in Cuba, life is so
full of surprises, it never occurred to me that he'd be inviting me
to come with him now..., no, hon, I don't go with him everywhere
because he goes off really early when I'm still sleepy, and anyway,
for me this is super-luxury that I want to enjoy, but when he comes
back, he always tells me about it, in the restaurant he spends all
his time telling me about the interviews and about so and so and
the others and so I'm finding out some things about his job, as I
said, this is a professional trip, he has to write an article about the
Moncada celebrations..., yes, yes, well, the 25th we went together
to the carnival parade they put on, really lovely, a shame you
missed it, of course we were in the foreign press section, you could
see everything perfectly from there, the whole city was celebrating,
Fabian took some photos, the dance groups were terrific, of course
they were carrying banners from carnivals of years past, because,
well, there's no cloth to make new ones, but in any case they
looked great and on the other side, the city was happy, you know?
and I had this really weird feeling, there I was surrounded by foreigners drinking Havana Club and smoking Camels, and on the
other side, a city full of people, singing and applauding their
favorite bands and dancers, because the carnival was competitive
and everyone looked happy, it's incredible how little you need to
be happy, people really need this, no one was thinking about all
the scarcities or about not having beer, everyone was cheering and
feeling good...don't tell me that, as though I were some dummy,
really, there was an atmosphere of happiness there, the first secretary of the Party was the one giving out prizes, and people were
yelling in his support and cheering him by name, I saw that myself,
don't you tell me that the five stars are going to my head, because
that's offensive..., no, I'm not getting angry, well, let's change the
subject, I'll tell you more about it, that afternoon was a lot of fun,
on the way back to the hotel we went to the café by the pool to eat
pizzas, and what pizzas, hon! without exaggerating, seriously, I
couldn't even finish it, then we stayed up drinking vodka martinis

for a while and went to sleep, since the next day we had to get up early..., vodka martini?...it's what Fabian drinks, instead of gin, vodka, it's marvelous, someday you can try it, you'll see, hon, we all get our turn, well, yesterday, the wake up call was at 4:00 A.M. because at five they stage the commemorative attack on the barracks, so we went down around 4:30 A.M. and at that hour, forget about it, there wasn't a single taxi at the hotel, a real offense, this man began to complain about it, but as you know employees around here couldn't care less about that, so anyway they told us how to get there on foot, fortunately it wasn't far, on the way I had to listen to a whole long speech, it's scandalous, do you realize what it means for a five star not to have taxis waiting at 4:30 in the morning? crazy, but we got there and it was really lovely, the kids acted out the assault, and then there was singing and dancing, revolutionary hymns, I got goose bumps, truly, and started snapping photos of everything I saw, it was as though I were really living forty years ago, except that now no one got killed or thrown into prison, it was just a wonderful experience...oh, sweetie, you're really impossible! if you'd been there, I'm sure you'd have felt the same way...no, it has nothing to do with the pizza or the hotel either, it was a moment I'm never going to forget, if you're going to be that way I'll stop telling you about it...okay, okay, when we got back I was really sleepy, so I drank some coffee and went back to bed, then in the afternoon, we had lobster for lunch and went to the pool, which is really nice, you can swim and there are no kids who bother you or people yelling, it's so-o-o peaceful, Fabian didn't swim, he sat at a little table talking to some journalists, French, I think, but since I don't understand any French, I kept on swimming and sunning myself...and drinking vodka martinis, of course, at around 7 P.M. we went up to the room, because the ceremony was at 8 and he wanted to watch it, pretty annoyed because he couldn't get them to give him a press pass, we bathed and he called room service to get something to eat, when I came out of the bath, I turned on the TV, there was a really good documentary about the tourist attractions all over the country, I found out about a whole bunch of hotels and villas I didn't know existed and they even showed our hotel, listen, this country is gorgeous, really, it was like I was watching a foreign film, but no, it was all sea, the summer breeze, the palm trees, Fabian says that when he comes back he's going to take me on a vacation and not a work trip, I'm already wanting like crazy for him to come back and he hasn't even left yet, oh honey!, what a beautiful country we have here...no, sweetie, it's not just on television, it's true, you need to meet up with a guy like this one to hear him talk and then you wouldn't be saying these things, he'd be smoking Camels and drinking vodka martinis but he keeps telling me about things that really scare me...yes, and well, now, I didn't get to see the end of the documentary because at a quarter of eight he switched channels to watch the speech, at that point room service came, we'd ordered pizzas, some beer and coffee, and then we stretched out to listen to the speech, they were saying really interesting things, Fabian was all excited, you know how he adores this country, he had me take some notes, and even though I was a little tired from swimming in the afternoon, I tried to write down all the sentences he repeated, fortunately it was a short speech, not like some other years, then we stayed there drinking beer and smoking, it all seemed really upbeat to me, very up to date, we're going through some hard times, but I know this country will weather it...enough already, hon, come on, stop teasing me! you know I don't like beer that much and I'm not dying for a pizza either, quite apart from all that, I liked the speech, yes, you have to understand that the country is going through a difficult period..., listen, you have to be here to know how it is, you probably didn't even hear the speech, Fabian has talked to me about so many things that I've begun to understand stuff I didn't see before, you think you can sum up life in a beer and a little food?...you're pretty ignorant of the world, girl! there are things that are more important and more essential than air conditioning..., yes, I know you don't have it and I don't either, but if you'd only been here, all you have to do is see people's faces on television and see how they shout and cheer, this is a great country, hon, dollars aren't everything..., no, I'm not trying to give you a second speech, it's just that it annoys me that you don't understand, hold on a second, I'm going to get a pack of cigarettes...no, don't worry about it, Fabian will pay for the call...listen...let me go on, when the speech was over the party at the hotel began, in the bar by the pool there are some little tables, they put a sound system out there and a band started playing, I laughed so hard, hon, we were sitting there and by the fourth vodka martini everything struck me as funny, if you'd seen the guys who were singing you'd have roared, some bumpkins in ridiculous shirts and a mulatto broad in skin-tight latex pants, hideous, one of those black women the Spanish like so much, the kind that cinches her belt really tight and doesn't care if the fat bulges over it, I don't know how people can be so vulgar and so badly dressed, hideous clothes and hairstyles that call out, "Laugh at me!"...it was so funny, Fabian and I both got so high we danced all the way to our room and called down for a bottle of vodka to keep partying, I don't know when we got to bed, today he got up and went off somewhere, he gets up early even when he's been up really late, but I don't, I stayed in bed and I have no idea when I got up, I took a shower, I called room service to bring me a full breakfast and a vodka martini, just to keep up the tradition, and then I thought I'd give you a call...yes, we're on a flight tomorrow morning, I don't know what we'll do today, the truth is I wish this Fortieth Anniversary of Moncada would go on forever...no, silly, it's not just because of the hotel, we've had a really good time and I've learned a lot of things, tomorrow Havana will be back to normal, the city full of people, we'll decide what to do in these last days Fabian has here, see if you can find yourself a friend who will treat you to a vodka martini, you'll love it...okay, hon, I have to let you go, we've talked for long enough and it's about time for the movie that I saw an ad for yesterday...yes, I'll call you as soon as I get there, oh, by the way, what have you been up to these days?...ah, okay...yes, yes, of course, the usual stuff, fine, it doesn't matter, we'll see what we can find to do there..., I'll let you go..., yes, okay...bye now...

Translated by Mary G. Berg.

Pied Piper Picked a Peck

Anna Lidia Vega Serova

1. KIKI

My mother lives in a big house with a pool. She sent the photos to Grandma. There were photos of the house, of my mom's dog, of Mr. Brown, of their children, of their cars, of the pool, and of what they have in the refrigerator. My mom married Mr. Brown, but he didn't want her to come get me. My brothers Tony and Johnny are twins and they're two years old. Each one has a tricycle with a horn on it and a plastic counter that shows how many miles they've gone. My mom has black eyes and black hair, too, and suntanned skin. She looks really pretty in the photos. When I close my eyes, I see her the way she is in the photos. But one time I dreamed about her the way she was when I knew her. We were swimming in the pool from the photos. She was laughing and saying to me, "Come to me, Kiki, come on," but I couldn't swim. We were separated by the water and I couldn't get to my mother. My mom's name is Marlén. I have a friend at school whose name is Marlén, too, and when her mom calls her to come eat and take a bath she yells: "Marle-e-én!" and it makes me shiver because I always think it's my mom who is being called, and I'm stuck there not knowing what to do. I was four years old (a little older than Tony and Johnny) when she left. They have tricycles and tennis shoes with little lights on them and their own room all decorated with cartoon characters. I always think of them when the cartoons are on TV. There's a photo of their room and of the two of them lying in twin beds in pajamas with little stars on them and my mom in a bathrobe sitting in a chair between the beds holding a big storybook. My mom didn't read me stories because she was always too busy, especially at night. Sometimes she'd be gone for a long time, a week or more. Or if not, she'd be doing her nails and her hair and then she'd put on perfume, get dressed and go off to work.

When I was very small, I got sick and my mom was at the hospital every day with me. But I don't remember that. That's what Grandma says. My grandma's name is Carmen and she's my dad's mother. Grandma believes in the saints and I don't know, but I think I've got special pacts with the warriors and with the hand of Orula. When we're celebrating the saints' days, Grandma pushes me toward the altar and says, "Ask." I always ask for the same thing: to live with my mom. When my mom left, she said she'd come and get me. She left with a girl named Juliana. I remember that because Juliana gave me clothes and toys and a Walkman that doesn't have batteries but I keep it in case someday I get batteries.

Before she left, my mom sold everything or gave it away, and she took some things to my grandparents who are her parents and live in Oriente. She asked me, "Who do you want to stay with, Grandma Carmen or Mima and Pipo?" I said I didn't want to stay with anyone, that I loved her. Grandma Carmen started crying and called her bad names and then I wanted to defend my mom and I hugged her but she pushed me away and I almost fell down. I don't know why she did that. Maybe she was afraid that if she showed she cared about me that I'd think she'd stay, but I only wanted to defend her because Grandma was being unfair to her, even though Grandma isn't bad, just very bitter. That's what my grandparents in Oriente say when I go there during vacations. Grandma's had a very hard life because my dad's in prison because he killed his dad who was my grandpa and my mom took off and left me behind and that puts a burden on Grandma. That's what my grandparents in Oriente say and they also say I should stay with them but I don't want to because they live in a house they share with my uncle. My grandma and grandpa get really upset when I go see my uncle, but I don't know why, my uncle gives me mangos and his wife gives me rice pudding, but Grandma yells at me and I don't want to live there even though I like Puerto Padre a lot and riding in a car and one day I got to pet a horse. I'd have liked to have a horse to ride, like Zorro with my black cape floating in the air. When my mom comes to get me, I'll ask her to buy me one. If Mr. Brown lets her. I don't think he is a good person, even though he's smiling a lot, playing trains with my brothers Tony and Johnny.

When my mom got to Miami she split up with Juliana right away and she went up north and fell in love with Mr. Brown. Juliana was really nice, she gave me a bunch of things and she told me, "You'll be joining us soon, I promise." I liked her even though Grandma wouldn't talk to her and called my mom bad names. Before she met Juliana, my mom used to go out to work every night and came home tired and in a bad mood with bags of things and at first Grandma would say, "I don't know why I have to put up with this shame." That was at first, but then she'd grab the bags, put the things away and when she wanted something, she'd say, "If we had a little flour, I'd make croquettes," or "See if you can find a little oil, we're running out." And Mom would come home the next day with flour or oil or whatever we needed. Grandma tells me about some things, but some I can remember. I remember when I met Juliana. My mom didn't usually take me to meet her foreign boyfriends. They probably didn't like kids. But Juliana was different. She had white hair cut really short like the fuzz on a bath towel, and light smiling eyes. She picked me up and said to me, "So you're Enrique!" And then she'd call me Enrique all the time or Enrique The Great, and not Kiki like everyone else did. And my mom looked happy and didn't go out to work every night, only when Juliana was in Cuba, until she left, but the last days I hardly saw her and Grandma used to cry a lot at night when she thought I was asleep and I listened to her and I thought my heart would break but I didn't know what to do. A lot of the time I don't know what to do and then I start saying over to myself, "Peter Piper picked a peck of pickled peppers" that a doctor Grandma took me to taught me, the one who asked me a lot of questions and had me draw things for him because I pee in my bed. It seems that it's because I keep remembering that dream about the swimming pool, because I always want to dream about Mom again so I can swim to where she is. She sent the photos with people who were coming here and she also sent money and Grandma bought lots of flowers for Saint Barbara and also bought me some tennis shoes but without lights and she said she didn't have enough for batteries for the Walkman, but I think what's going on is that she doesn't want to spend money on stupid things and she thinks those are stupid things. If she'd let me, I'd buy a jar of mayonnaise, the biggest one I could find, and a whole can of soda crackers so I could eat crackers with mayonnaise until I was full. It's the first thing I'm going to ask Mom when she takes me with her. And I'm also going to ask her for a gun that squirts soap bubbles and tennis shoes with lights and a horse and one more thing that I've been thinking about for a long time. I'm going to wait until Mr. Brown isn't around, or my brothers, because I feel embarrassed about it, and then I'm going to ask her to read me a story. Grandma says I'm doing badly in school because I daydream all the time, but the truth is that I have a lot of things to think about and also that every day I get into a fight with someone because people think that if they live with their moms and dads they are better than me. When my mom comes to get me they're going to have to eat their words. I don't like school much and when my mom takes me away I'm not going to study any more, what I want to do is be a boxer so I'll be really strong and can knock out anyone who messes with me or with my mom. And I'll defend Tony and Johnny, too. At first I didn't like them much, but then I thought about how they're really little and they're sure to need a brother to protect them. I'm going to take care of them, and I'm going to help my mom. I help Grandma Carmen, I take the trash out, I clean the fish and I do other things, because I'm the man of the house. Grandma says that when my dad was a boy, he used to do these things. She has photos of him and also of my grandpa, the one I never got to know because my dad killed him. I don't know why he did that. Grandma doesn't want to talk about it. I don't remember my dad, but in the photos he looks cheerful and strong. I'd have liked to get to know him, and for him to know me. Grandma says when she comes from seeing him, that he asks about me and sends kisses. Sometimes I wonder what it would be like if my mom and dad lived with me, but it leaves me not knowing what to do and I start repeating, "Peter Piper picked a peck of pickled peppers..." Grandma Carmen says a lot of bad things about my mom and my Oriente grandparents say bad things about my dad and I love them all very much.

2. MARLÉN

I couldn't stand living with my parents any longer; if I hadn't married Enrique, I'd have slit my wrists. They were all upset about the house and they nearly threw out my brother and his pregnant wife and their kid, nearly put them out on the street. Luckily, he got stubborn and then they put up the wall right across the hall-way. It's the most ridiculous thing I've ever seen: the living room, the bedroom, the bath, and then a wall. They cook in the living room. On the other side they have a bedroom, the kitchen and the patio. They do their business in the patio, over the drain. But that was after I escaped. At that point, I was in high school, which I never finished, and living in the midst of that ongoing war, I nearly went out of my mind. I liked Enrique and besides, he was from Havana. The problem was with his parents.

His mother is a bitter sourpuss and his father was an alcoholic. They had hardly any furniture, he'd drunk everything up, and besides that, he'd get into huge rows that made you want to run out of there. We tried to stay out of each other's way, we'd close ourselves into our bedroom or we'd go out places, but it wasn't easy. Carmen, my mother-in-law, hated me from the moment she laid eyes on me. I kept trying to help her, to keep the house more or less decent, but she'd stop me and say, "This is my house." I'd put out a knick-knack and she'd stick it back in my bedroom, and on it went, until I gave up. But on the other hand she always wanted me to clean and scrub and do the wash and then it was always, "This is how I make the croquettes," or "I always iron Enriquito's shirts this way." And Enrique didn't say a word. Instead of backing me up he'd say, "She's my mother; you have to respect her." I thought nothing could be worse than my own home. But the truth is that it's harder to put up with insults from people you don't know. I'd have left if I hadn't been pregnant already. I'd have gotten rid of it, but Enrique had such a tantrum that it wasn't easy. He made a little money working as a lathe operator. I started to get together supplies for the baby by myself. It never went through Carmen's head to offer to help, but it's better that way: I don't owe her anything. My father-in-law was having more and more drinking problems, twice he beat up on Carmen. Enrique had to put up with it. I had saved up some money for a crib and my father-in-law took it. I told Carmen about it and she looked right through me as if I weren't there, all but shrugging her shoulders. Enrique was at work. His father rolled in, high as a kite, I asked him for my baby's money and he said, "I didn't take anything," and, "I don't know anything about any money." Carmen went off to market, I was crying in the kitchen, and what does the old man do but come from behind me and grab my ass. My belly was huge by then but he couldn't have cared less, he started pawing me. I tried to get away, I didn't even know when Enrique got there, I was screaming under my father-in-law's weight and he was sticking it in between my legs. I only felt myself being yanked away, it was Enrique, he had the knife in his hand. He was out of his mind with rage, he stabbed his father seven times, killed him like a hog. At that point Carmen came in, she threw herself on the old man swimming in blood, the loaves of bread fell into the blood, and then she leapt up at Enrique and I held her back and Enrique turned livid, looked at us weirdly, ran over to the balcony and threw himself over the rail. After all that, anything can happen. Nothing scares me anymore. Enrique didn't kill himself, they took him to the emergency room and covered him almost entirely in a plaster cast. They took me to the hospital, too, because I started bleeding and had problems with blood pressure. I stayed in the hospital until I gave birth. My mother had to come from Puerto Padre because Carmen was taking care of Enrique who by sheer luck wasn't seriously injured.

All the court proceedings and that stuff, she had to get through on her own. I expected to take the baby home with me, but my mother asked, "And where do you think you're going to put the crib?" Carmen came to see me once, and she said, "It was all your fault. I don't want you in my house." That made me so furious that I decided to go back to her house after all. I had the right, she couldn't throw me out and especially not with a baby. When Enriquito was born I had such a hard time, I thought I was dying. But no, I got out of the hospital, thank God the baby had come out fine, and we went back to that house. Carmen wouldn't speak to me. My mother went back to Oriente, to continue her battles with my brother and his wife. Before she left she said to me, "If you want, come along with me and we'll figure something out," but there was no way I was going to give that pleasure to my miserable mother-in-law. At first it was awful. The baby cried a lot, he didn't let me get any sleep, then there were all his diapers, and my breasts were drying up. I'd been putting him to sleep in a washbasin, but luckily some neighbors loaned me a crib. My mother-in-law spent her days half asleep, rocking in her rocking chair. I was about to do something really crazy, out of sheer frustration, but I controlled myself. I went to see Enrique in prison a couple of times. But he pushed me over the edge when he said, "The baby

is your responsibility, make sure you take good care of him so you'll
have a clear conscience. And you have to take care of my mother."
I walked out and never went back. He made me furious. And
besides, I wasn't attracted to him any longer. I had to work hard
selling rum and cigarettes in order to pay for milk and rice. Luckily
Panchito, the next door neighbor, took an interest in me and
helped me along. It was a bit of help, anyway, and it didn't cost me
much. When I got enough money together, I divorced Enrique. I
thought Pancho was serious about us, but he was just killing time.
Well, never mind, he pulled me out of a deep hole. At that point,
Carmen turned to religion and took up *santería*, or witchcraft, or
lord knows what, and she started doing spells and throwing
potions on me, but they only affect people who believe in that
stuff, and I'm way past being scared by anything like that. I kept
on going out with Pancho and with other guys in the neighborhood. I wouldn't say anything to Carmen, I'd get dressed, go out,
and leave it at that. Otherwise she wouldn't look after the kid for
me, and how was I going to get money and food together? At first
she'd yell at me that she wasn't going to take on anyone else's bur-
dens and worse things, but she seemed to grow fond of Kiki. The
truth is that the kid was thriving in spite of everything. I realized
that I was keeping my distance from him. I tried to be loving and
all, but I just couldn't, even though I forced myself to think about
him, and when I started going out with foreigners, I'd ask for
things for the kid, the treats that he liked. The first time I went
out with a foreigner was by chance. I was hitchhiking, he picked
me up, and he invited me to eat, and I realized what a lot I'd been
missing out on. In time I took it seriously, like any other job. There
were some guys I liked, but none of them offered me anything permanent and I decided to get the hell out of the country before I
got old, fat and ugly living in that squalor, in that swamp that swallows people up. I looked at myself in the mirror and thought I
looked pretty sexy, especially when I put on shorts and a tight top
and took care with my makeup. "What's all this for?" I wondered,
and then I just wanted to scream: "All I can look forward to is
spending my whole life in this hole with a woman who detests me,

with a child who depresses me, with no future whatsoever, until I get old, fat and ugly and no one will look at me." One day I cried so much my eyes were swollen so I couldn't go out, and Kiki ran his hand over my hair and I felt so sorry for him and for myself and even for Carmen, that I could have slit my wrists. I hugged him and told him, "I love you Kiki," and I think I did really care for him and I played with him, I taught him how to say some tongue-twisters, he couldn't pronounce all those Ps in Peter Piper and we laughed a lot, but then I got bored and I left him with Carmen and went off. I don't know why I remember that day so clearly. He has my black eyes and his father's face, with funny looking ears that stick out. Carmen sent me a photo of him, and he's really grown up now. But there's a sadness in his eyes. I have no regrets; I did what I had to do, there was no option. I know I'm a good mother, I never mistreated him and he never lacked for anything. I left him with Carmen knowing he'd be well cared for, otherwise I'd never have gone. And if I could take him with me, I would, but Enrique won't sign the release, he says that only if I get him out, too, and I could never do that, my husband would never do that, nor would I want to, I left in order to forget about him and about all that happened, and if he were here I couldn't. I managed to get myself out, I'm happy, I have everything: a family, a good house, two great sons, clothing, food. My whole past there is like a nightmare, like something that happened to someone else or in a movie. My husband talks sometimes about one day going to see my parents and Kiki, but I feel a wave of nausea when I imagine returning to Cuba, to that divided house or to Havana, walking through streets where I suffered so much, and seeing the faces of Carmen and Kiki, having him ask me something I don't know how to answer. Seeing all those people who used to call me whore and slut and prostitute. But no one has walked in my shoes. I hooked up with Juliana only because she was the first and only one who said to me: "I'm going to get you out," and she did get me out. And she was a good person, except that I had to really struggle to be with her, because it revolted me to be with a woman. But as a friend she was terrific, too bad the break up was so messy, she just never understood that if I'd tricked her and used her, it was because I had no option. When we met, I couldn't imagine it. And then I asked myself, "Why not?" For sure, no man ever treated me with such attention and affection. She wanted to know everything about me, she met Kiki and Carmen and she was kind to everyone. She asked,, "What do you need?" If I'd asked her for an elephant, she'd have gotten me one. All I had to do was sleep with her and kiss her. Though even in that she was very tactful, she'd talk to me as though I were a teenager, and she didn't get furious when I didn't want to do something. But I put on a good show and I went out of my way to please her in everything, I couldn't lose my big chance. And to avoid hassles and gossip, I was up front about it: "I'm with a woman because I choose to be, and I don't care what anyone thinks." In less than six months, I left. Juliana paid good money to get me out, we had a marriage ceremony, we took a huge number of photos. I know she's never going to forgive me. When we got to Miami, I leveled with her, because I really respected her, and she turned pale and said, "I could really fuck you up but I care too much about you. Get out, I never want to see you again." There I was alone in a foreign country, but I'm used to struggling. Before I left, I'd been given lots of addresses, I looked at a map to find the farthest place, and I went there. They found a job for me right away, then I hooked up with Brown who is rolling in money and isn't a bad sort. I had a lot of luck and I think I deserved it. I sent the photos to my dear mother-in-law so she could burst with envy, and so that Kiki would remember me, children forget everything so quickly. I have my life and I'm happy, but if Kiki were with me, I'd feel more reassured at night when I start remembering it all and I can't sleep and I take pills and I keep thinking. I'm going to get wrinkles from thinking so much.

3. CARMEN

Oh blessed Saint Barbara, send sleep to that boy who is tossing in his bed, little angel, nothing is his fault, nor mine, in this miserable life full of catastrophes, send me health and the strength to finish bringing him up, poor little orphan, and give him health and energy, and for his father, too, who ruined his life all because of that tramp he brought from the countryside, no Havana girl was good enough for him, a city full of good and decent girls, but no, he had to go looking for a wretch who disgraced us all and then went off to enjoy the high life and never gave a thought to the baby she stuck my son with who probably isn't even his, but it's not the poor boy's fault and he doesn't have anyone but me, because his country grandparents don't take care of him, or give a hoot how he is, off on their farm out there, all they do is fight with their son to get rid of him like they got rid of their bitch of a daughter who is the most shameless hussy I've ever met in my life. She pretended to be so saintly at first, with her, "I bought you this ashtray," and, "How about putting this little doily here?" as if I needed her ashtrays and her garbage! She was quick enough to get pregnant, of course, sucking poor Enriquito dry, holed up in their bedroom all the time and getting some on the side, too, thanks to the old man, may he rest in peace, going out in those scandalous Lycra outfits, showing off her treasures to the whole world, of course he had to mess with her, she set it up herself to get my son sent to prison and then screw around with everyone, I don't know why she didn't catch one of those AIDS things, not even illnesses stick to her, she's so bad, pure poison. Never in my life have I hurt anyone, I don't know what I did to deserve this. I always worked like a mule, from age fourteen on, when I got married, taking care of the house and of my husband, who had a drinking problem but in every other way was a good man and a hard worker, and if a shelf had to be hung or tiles set, he'd do all the household repairs; and my floors were so clean you could have seen your reflection in them, and my sheets, why people would ask me what I did to get my sheets so white, and my husband was always ahead of the pack, he was the first to be given a refrigerator, he even took Enriquito to voluntary service jobs, and Enriquito was really good in school, too, and he was doing a man's job. He deserved better luck. And I broke my back taking care of him, trying to give him a future, I spent so much time teaching him and nursing him back to health, because he was sickly, always wanting the best for him, and he was always good and kind, and all those girlfriends he had, hard working, honest, decent, and all to end up with a lazy tramp, who doesn't even know how to iron a shirt, or scrub the floor, or take care of her husband. What should a mother do when she can see that her son has married a no-good woman? He'd go off to work and she'd be out of the house in a flash, day after day, and there's even more, several times I caught her coming out of the bathroom naked, as if my husband were blind, or she'd sit down to watch television just wearing a T-shirt, crossing her legs, the shameless hussy. And then she makes a big fuss when the old man goes after her! I told Enriquito about it and he gave me that run around about arteriosclerosis. When besides her keeping him on a leash like a tame lamb, he'd never washed a dish or taken out the garbage, but with her, he'd even wash out her underpants when I wasn't there and I'd say to him, "She's really got you under her thumb, you fool, throw out that worthless floozy," and he'd talk back to me, he who'd always been respectful all his life, and just because of that tramp, who was whooping it up while he was going all out for us. I even had to fix the coffee in the mornings because the princess wanted to sleep until noon! And no one could tell her anything because right away she made sour faces saying, "I'm going back home," and then she'd argue with Enrique who'd be crawling on the floor to kiss her feet. Seeing his son so helpless, of course his father drank even more and she was just waiting for this to stir up more trouble. She invented that about the money. Neither I nor anyone else in my family would ever dare take anything from anyone else, we'd die first. But she used to spend every penny my son gave her, money he'd earned with blood and sweat, and she'd squander it on pizzas and ice cream. Poor little thing, her big belly gave her cravings! And then, at the hour of truth, she blamed it all on the old man, I don't know why he didn't give her a good thwacking. Then she started to lead him on, moving her ass around almost naked, and the man lost his head, I almost lost my son, too, but if he had listened to me from the beginning, all these disasters might never have happened. She tried to finish me off, too, to take over the house and all my things, that was her intention, but she couldn't do it. I consulted a *babalao*, and he read the cards and told me, "Bad things are being done to you." And who by, if not that witch? But I began to turn it all around. She'd attack me and I'd give it back to her twofold, and she was the one who had to leave.

And let's hope she doesn't come back, for God's sake. I'm going to show the boy how to be a decent citizen and little by little he'll start forgetting that tramp, who never loved him or took care of him. His diapers were all yellow because she didn't even know how to wash and then she'd go out and leave him howling while she went off with just anyone and even with women, may God forgive me. The truth is that she brought back all kinds of things, and we never lacked lard or soap or toys for the boy, but how can a mother be replaced by candy and junk? A mother should be with her son and not go off when he's filthy and crying without a clean diaper. She took advantage, because she knew that I wouldn't leave him without a bottle of milk, she was selfish, just out for herself. She thought only about clothes and perfume and nightclubs instead of keeping up a good face for her husband, whom she sent off to prison just as she sent mine to the grave, that viper, leaving me alone in my old age and poisoning me little by little, unloading that innocent boy on me, who is not a burden, but whose head is full of fantasies about his mother and all the time he's saying, "My mom" here and, "My mom" there, and his real mother is me, even though I didn't give birth to him, but at least I didn't abandon him, and he has been my only consolation during these years. And now she has the nerve to send that stack of photos of that house and those kids and cars, probably all someone else's. I know how it works, they have their photo taken beside some car and even husbands and children, and then claim they are theirs, when in fact they're just barely scraping by. I hope that's how it is, she'd certainly deserve it, for all the havoc she's wrought. It's the boy I feel really bad about. He's got problems and he sits around like a dope, sometimes you have to shake him, it's as though he's in a trance and starts babbling nonsense, those tongue-twisters, and he wets his bed at night and he's such a good child, bless him.

I'm not so well either, I have to take pills because I burst into tears at any little thing, I'm old. Enrique says to me, "Take care of yourself, Mami, and take care of the boy, I can find one like her anywhere," but the poor little guy is so thin and I think he's sick, he coughs a lot and I hope it's nothing bad, because I can't bear any more tragedies, I've had it. Ever since he brought her here, I knew she was a bird of ill omen, you could see it on her face and in the way she behaved, she was slippery like a snake where there's no way to get ahold of it, never looking you in the eye, hiding her eyes all the time so you never know what she's thinking. I wasn't wrong, either, she even took up with women, as if it weren't enough to cuckold my son with any guy who crossed her path; and no doubt there's more, they say people even do it with dogs these days. If she'd at least had the tact to do this filth discreetly, but no, she spread it all over the neighborhood that she'd become a lesbian so I wouldn't be able to look people in the eye, and besides that, she had the gall to bring that brazen bull-dyke into my house, who arrived laden with gifts, as though gifts could cover up the shame of it. I didn't say a word to her, if I'd said anything, I'd have screamed insults. I couldn't even stand to look at her. My heart did flips when I saw that dyke pick up the child and give him chocolates and things. I don't know why it didn't make him sick, but he's not my son, all I could do was close myself up in my room and cry, I was burning so inside, from pain and anguish. "I can't cope with this," I said to myself, but I had to put up with it because I'm the one responsible for the little angel and he needs me. Thank heaven nobody in the neighborhood said anything to me because even at my age I'd have had to smash someone's teeth in because of that whore, but still, I started looking around for a new place, and then it was Enrique who said, "No, you're not going to move and start over again in a new place. You're not the one to blame." And it's true, people know me, they know I'm a decent person, not some shameless slut. If I didn't kick her out it was for the child's sake, so she wouldn't take him away to suffer neglect or hunger, better that I should suffer instead, he already has enough pain ahead of him when he grows up and finds out that his mother is a whore and a dyke who abandoned him. He'll be told the whole story, for sure.

I'm going to take care of him and bring him up and make a man out of him, and that viper better not even dream of taking him away ever, she's already done him enough damage. If it ever occurs to her to come back here someday, she isn't going to set foot inside this door, and I'll tell the boy loud and clear, "I'm your real mother, I'm the one who sacrificed for your sake, not that bitch, damn her."

4. OPTIONAL SCENE

A tourist taxi stops in front of the building. Out steps a beautiful black haired woman dressed in an elegant gray suit. She walks back to the trunk. The taxi driver helps her with her luggage. People begin to gather around her, others call from the balconies: "Mar-le-eén! Mar-le-én!" The woman smiles, abashed, greets them and answers questions, while her anxious eyes look up at balconies and faces until she sees the older woman who comes down the stairs in a hurry, drying her hands on her apron, exclaiming emotionally,, "Oh, blessed Saint Barbara, thank God she is here! She finally came back!" The young woman rushes toward her and hugs her tightly. The two burst into tears. The neighbors help with the suitcases, they go up the stairs asking questions and interrupting each other, everyone in an ecstasy of joy and surprise. When they get to the apartment, the young woman in gray drops her arm from around the old woman's shoulders and swoops up a boy age ten or so, who is standing in the doorway watching with sad black eyes. She embraces him crying and covers him with kisses, while he keeps muttering to himself: "Peter Piper picked a peck of pickled peppers."

Translated by Mary G. Berg.

Russian Food

Anna Lidia Vega Serova

To Milanés [1]

I wanted to see Ana, but I wasn't sure Ana wanted to see me. In general, you don't ask this question, you just go over and see whoever it is you want to see. But it's different with Ana because Ana is different. When she doesn't want to see people, she doesn't open the door. This is pretty depressing if you're standing there knocking and she doesn't open up.

I left it to chance: if I found cabbage along the way, I'd go, if not, I'd go somewhere else. The cabbage is an old joke. Ana said she'd love to cook me a Russian meal but she didn't have the ingredients. She has everything except cabbage. Ana is half Russian and a marvelous cook. The truth is that she's a marvelous whatever-she-does, but her cooking is out of this world. Once she invited a

---

[1] Milanés. Modesto Milanés is a friend I care about and respect a lot. He helped me when I was beginning to write. He used to come by my house, we'd drink tea or rum, we'd talk about literature and life. He no longer comes.

bunch of people over for her wedding anniversary to eat a whole assortment of great things. That was when she was married. She isn't any longer. Now she's free and that's a good thing. People can try their luck. Anyone can win the raffle. If she opens the door for you, of course.

I wandered around a fair amount looking for cabbage. In fact, I explored the whole circuit of vegetable stalls. But you could say I was just strolling around before I went to pay a call, breathing in oxygen, meditating about the meaning of life, observing nature in its urban habitat. There was quite a variety of vegetable habitats. But none of them included cabbage.

Why do Russians have such a passion for cabbage? Russians are an odd breed. They all descend from czars who ate sturgeon, caviar, black bread and cabbage.

When Ana speaks of the Russians she rolls her eyes all the way up until you can see the whites.

"Oh, oh," she exclaims, "Snowflakes, chestnuts in bloom, the cherry orchards!"

It doesn't become her at all, because you can't see her pupils.

"Oh, Oh!" she exclaims. "The Hermitage, the Master and Margarita, Moscow Does Not Believe in Tears," and tears drip from her Muscovite blue eyes.

Then everyone runs around looking for cabbages. "Don't cry, dear, alas we can't offer you sturgeon or caviar... But on our behalf, please accept the best intentions of international solidarity in their culminating materialization as cabbages." And Ana would fix a borscht. She adds salt, onion and a bay leaf. She invites the entire neighborhood. She bakes black bread and passes it out to the hungriest.

I don't want your black bread, Ana, I'm hungry for you, for your half Russian soul. In response, Ana grabs the guitar and belts out *ochi chornie, ochi strastnie...* or a *troika* or a *kazachok...* I don't much like the idea of spending the whole day looking for non-existent cabbages. I could buy flowers. What flowers do Russians like? Ana rolls her eyes when she speaks of poppies. And of poppyseed juice made with pharmaceutical care and injected into a vein.

Because Ana had a dark and depraved history in the suburbs of St. Petersburg. She was involved with picturesque people from the underworld. She tells lots of stories about her early days between one cabbage and the next.[2]

Lettuce won't do. Or Swiss chard or watercress or asparagus. The entry ticket has got to be cabbage, I say. And the cross-eyed vegetable seller wearing an apron and a cap tells me about the truck that made deliveries in Zone 24 this morning. Before I even take in what I'm hearing, I'm running, jumping over the zone dividers (one, two, three, who cares how many) let's just hope there are still some left. Ana, I'll find them, just you wait, and we'll eat to the sound of *Swan Lake* or whatever you choose. I'm all set to listen to all the *Alla Pugacheva* you want, and all your stories about troubled times on the banks of the Neva, I can even put up with the eighteen photo albums, but please, only let there be..., please...

Here are the cabbages. Real, gorgeous. Fifty centavos each. Three! No, I'll take four! Yes, give me four. What on earth are you going to do with four cabbages? Into Ana-the-Russian's stew pots. Baked cabbage. Cabbage salad. Stuffed cabbage leaves. Borscht, cabbage soup. Ana washes them, separates the leaves, chops them, shreds them. (Cabbage cream soup, breaded fried cabbage, grilled cabbage). Ana rushes around muttering magic words in her pagan language, she stirs, seasons, sautés. (Cabbage croquettes, cabbage marmalade, cabbage pies, cabbage juice).

I put them into my knapsack. Only two will fit. I carry the other two in my hands. Ana, open the door for me. It's me, Potts, the mailman. Just kidding, you're the one with the pots, I've got the raw material. She offers me tea. Porcelain cups, samovar, wood in the stove, snowflakes through the window. Mashenka and the bear. Oh yes, tell me again about how you used to bathe in holes cut in the ice of the frozen river! Ana blows on her tea, sips, and

[2] I did invite Milanés to come over and eat borscht once. But he arrived late, the borscht was cold, and he didn't care for it.

rolls up her pupils so the whites of her eyes show.[3]

Open up, please. I have two cabbages in my pack and two more clutched against my chest with my right arm. I knock on the door with my left hand. "O-PEN A-NA!!" The neighbor comes out. "Ma'am, would you like me to give you a cabbage?"

"I don't know if anyone's there. I came out to see what all the racket was about."

Racket was me, availing myself of my legitimate rights. "Look, do you have a pen so I can leave a note?"

"A pen?"

"Yes ma'am, pens are those little tubes with other little ink-filled tubes in them, and you use them for..."

"Let me see if I can find a pencil, son..."

Ana is like this, she could care less that you've walked for miles, she opens up when she feels like it and when she doesn't, she goes off to get together with her half Russian -or totally Russian- friends, and they drink vodka and sing *Katiusha*. Ana can wander around wherever she feels like going, telling incredible stories about drugs, sex and violence, rolling her blue eyes so you see the whites, sighing her endlessly Slavic sigh, and here I am with four cabbages like outdated lunch tickets...

I bite into the cabbage I'm holding right under my chin. I chew, swallow, and take another bite.

"Here, son, I found a pencil stub, but it doesn't have a point and I don't have anything to sharpen it with, because if I were to use a kitchen knife for that, you can just imagine..., but don't keep pounding on that door, you're going to break it. And do you eat cabbage like that, just like a rabbit?"

---

[3]But other people who come over to my house have been able to appreciate my culinary gifts. What my friends liked best was not a Russian meal but a Colombian dish: rice with coconut, fish and garlic croutons. Yummmm!

Translated by Mary G. Berg.

Oh, Life

Adelaida Fernández de Juan

Oh, life, if I could only
live happiness
(...)
My hours of anguish
without you.
Oh, oh, oh life,
don't slip away
I know you've grasped it
with such sublime intensity.

—Yáñez and Gómez
(Beny Moré's creation)

She awoke in the middle of the night with a start that always surprised her, even though it happened all the time. It had been eight years now since she'd slept soundly, since before the birth of the first of her three sons. By now she was used to Simon's night cough, to Antonio's colic and to the dawn asthma attacks of Emilio, her youngest and favorite son, who slept in her bed because at any moment, said he with a three year old's irrefutable conviction, a monster might come looking for him. Simon, sturdy and confident, had the bed over by the door and slept with a wooden sword so he could fight off the pirates. Antonio, the only one in a crib, held tight to a little fire truck, worn out after putting out fires all day. Although her husband didn't insist that she be there for him at night, he didn't help her, either: "That's why you're not working, so you can take care of the kids."

The days were exhausting. She was almost permanently on call in the kitchen, powdered milk warmed with unrefined sugar for the grandparents, unsweetened coffee for her husband, evaporated milk for Simon, fresh cow's milk for Antonio, and a cup of yogurt for Emilio. She got whatever was left over; there was no time to be choosy. By the time she picked up after breakfast, it was time to start lunch. She'd begin cooking the rice (without salt, for the grandparents), beans (but not black ones, because of Emilio's asthma), and the protein (*po-treen* Simon called it) of the day, almost always boiled eggs. "Army rations again, woman?" "What do you want me to do? If I don't do the cooking first thing, the gas goes off, or the electricity, and then there's no time for anything."

Grandma dropped Simon off at school, the only task she'd been willing to do, and only as long as they all thanked her profusely every day when she got back. Antonio went with his father, who also picked him and Simon up in the afternoon, while Emilio stayed home with her, because his asthma didn't clear up until mid-morning when the sun was up. From the moment she got out of bed, she raced against the clock. Picking up the toys, crayons, shoes, skates and newspaper cutouts the kids had strewn all over the house the day before. Tidying the grandparents' room, throwing out the cigarette butts and making the big king-size bed with its long pillow that extended across the entire width of the bed. She always allowed herself the brief luxury of stretching out on that extravagant surface, rolling from side to side, even if just for five minutes (*life is eternal in five minutes*, in Beny's song), to imagine what it must be like to sleep in such a spacious place and have it all to herself, without sons or husband, exquisitely alone. After smoothing out the sheets and pulling up the bedspread, antique linen, from the olden days, "when your grandfather and I got married, dear, when everything was orderly, not a mess like now," she ran to the bathroom and pulled out the blue bucket to dump in the socks, the underpants, the shirt Antonio had splattered with watercolor paint, the tee shirt Simon threw up on yesterday afternoon, the pants Emilio got dirty in his struggle not to swallow his medicine, "it tastes like tennis shoes, Mom," and the greasy work clothes worn by her husband, a first class mechanic.

Before the sun had even come out, she would be in Juan Sebastián's patio, called that ever since they'd gotten a dog, Juan Sebastián, in order to please the kids. They had to close him up there because the coughs, the colics, and the asthma problems got so much worse that they couldn't let him loose in the rest of the house. Finally, the dog ran away, fed up with so much rejection and although the boys cried at first, they were consoled when their grandfather promised to convert the patio into a fish tank for them and eventually bring them an enormous whale who'd be named Moby Dick.

While she washed the clothes and soaked the urine stained sheets, she felt peacefully content. With the sky as audience, she sang her favorite song as she always did to gather her strength and be able to carry on with the dull routine allotted her by life. *As in a dream, you just suddenly appeared, what bliss, and that same marvelous night, you gave me a kiss.* She just had time for the first part of the song, Emilio was calling her from his room: "Mom yogurt in a cup, and put on my shoes without laces so I can read books." At last, she said, I can clean that room.

Always thinking about how to economize and later "we'll see," her husband had decided they would sleep in single beds so they could pass them on to two of the boys when they got bigger. They'd only buy one crib to pass on from child to child and when Antonio grew, they brought in Aunt Elisa's little antique bed, since she was already in the nursing home. And so, the room the grandparents had painted pink when the first grandchild was about to be born ("Let's hope it's a girl, dear, to keep you company in your old age, and let's call her María to keep on good terms with Our Lord.") had become a bunk room, with two twin beds and another similar one, and an elegant mahogany crib, "you can tell it's antique, dear."

"A good thing Emilio sleeps with you, honey, otherwise we wouldn't know where to put that fussy kid." Her husband didn't put up with the slightest sign of weakness, and "he's only three years old, sweetheart, don't be so hard on him." "You've got to start with training and behavior right when they're born, honey, don't argue with me about that one." "Yes, dear, you're right, that's why it's better if he sleeps with me, we'll see about that later on, as you say."

She worried about the possible incestuous impulses the boy might feel as he got older, or the frustration or maybe even violence that might surface in his adult life. Murderers and madmen in the movies always break down crying in the end and say it was their mothers' faults that they did this, that if their mothers had only done this, that if their mothers had only done that; anyway, there was something terrible and fascinating in the fact that Emilio slept with her, and when she made love with her husband, locking themselves in the bathroom when there were cartoons on TV, she felt guilty, as if she were cheating on her kids, especially on Emilio. The night she awakened suddenly, she felt oddly anxious, because Simon had not coughed, Antonio had not complained about colic, and Emilio's chest wasn't whistling when he breathed. Her husband was snoring, but that noise wasn't one that triggered alarm signals, so that shouldn't be why she'd wakened, either. She didn't want to move from her bed. The slightest movement could disturb the calm of that space, the peace she had achieved with such effort, so she put her ideas in motion, hoping that they wouldn't make a lot of noise.

Let's see, she thought, what is it I'm really worrying about. Did I forget to do something? Grandparents' room — cigarette butts — bed — double pillow. All done. Bathroom — faucets turned off — clothes washed, shoes picked up. All fine. Tomorrow's milks, Emilio's yogurt and cup, Antonio's homework, Simon's mitt and ball, for sports day. All there. Emilio's medicine set out for tomorrow, her husband's tool box, the basket of empty bottles for Grandpa for tomorrow, remind Grandma of her dentist appointment, all in order. Could I be worried about money? No, so far, thanks to the merciful Lord, as Grandpa says, and to the fact that my husband organizes everything so well, as Grandma says, we haven't had problems. It's just that I'd like to buy each boy a bicycle, but my husband says I'm out of my mind. What we should do, as a matter of principle, is to buy a second-hand bike (by that I understand cheap) for Simon, with training wheels so Antonio could ride it, too. And what about Emilio, I asked. "He can wait a while. There's an old scooter here, he can use that." Yes, dear, whatever you say. It's a question of means, even though you say it's principles.

Could it be that I'm going to die tomorrow? What if I vanish forever pretty soon, or in the next few hours? It must be that. I've wakened because surely life wants me to say farewell before I leave; it's my chance to do whatever I want, after all these years.

How difficult. I don't know what I want. Make an effort. Close your eyes and soar: everyone has wishes and you can't be so vain as to think you're the exception.

I'll give it a try. I'd like to have smooth, thick, silky hair like that blond who sings in the ABBA band. Come on, be more assertive: this is your one and only chance to ask for the impossible. Imagine that this is your last night on earth. What do you say?

I think I'd choose to have a slender body, with a totally clear complexion and tapering hands, small feet, and how would I like my back to be? What you're asking for is youth. We won't make any deals; after Faust, it would hardly be original. It still doesn't seem like much of a wish. You must have something more momentous to request. Yes. Forgiveness. Of whom? Of a close friend I had. If she was such a close friend, she's already forgiven you. Besides, everyone repents mistakes at the very end. Think of something less trite.

Solitude, then. I've wanted to be completely alone, without having to worry about anyone, but I immediately feel guilty because it must be a sin to wish that others would just disappear.

You're too lacking in faith to be a true atheist (there you are, harping on faith again, faith as requisite chapter and verse, and you're still a bundle of fears). You'll have your solitude, girl, the terrible solitude you yearn for is something you've always carried within you. I offer you the dreams you've lacked. Would you like to stroll down the Seine? See Venice in a gondola? Pyramids, waterfalls, snowfields, jungles? Perhaps catacombs, Big Ben, straight and leaning towers, bridges, deserts, gardens, volcanoes? I'd like to bathe nude, with the body I requested, in the dark waves of Havana's Malecón. Something that simple? You could have done that anytime at all. I've never had time. Let me do it now and then let me die there. I want the fear of the water to soak into me and the night's silence just across from my city to make me believe that happiness exists. I can't believe that your last wishes just extend the limited flight of your pale existence. I was expecting you to ask for a passionate love affair with a prolonged moment of pleasure you may never have felt. You're mistaken. I'd be content to make love with my usual partner, but if you insist I experience the passion you think I need, then let it be in a king-size bed like the grandparents', with white sheets, set in the middle of a deserted sandy beach, in the sunlight of a winter's day. Dear child, there's not much daylight in winter, but I applaud your burst of imagination. Suppose that you don't have much time left: are you missing anything important, a wish that has never been satisfied?

Yes, I'd like, just for tonight, to have all those who have gone, return. The dead, child? No, I've reconciled myself to those losses. I mean the ones who've gone off, who are like the semi-dead. I'd like to have my semi-dead return during this hour of semi-life, even if only to tell them I haven't forgotten them.

Again, you're asking for what you already have; no better company exists than the imaginary, child; no one has semi-died. If you'd looked closely at your hands, you'd see the hands of others there. I concede you one final wish: a request really worthy of you.

In that case, I'll only ask for the strength of your constancy. Remain in me, oh life; I don't want you to deprive me of the pleasure of my griefs, of the suffering of my bouts of sleeplessness, or of the anxiety that I will run out of time without even knowing what I want. Stay on, then, because my weak nature could not bear to cope with the grief of not seeing the sun as it rises.

Translated by Mary G. Berg.

Journey to Pepe

Adelaida Fernández de Juan

Everything we did
The lie and the truth
Everything we did is still
Alive somewhere;
little by little, everything
stops mattering.

—Fito Páez
Behind the Wall
of Lamentation.

Someone mentioned Celanova and she remembered that that was the place Pepe had said he'd be going. She called his house and they told her that after three moves they'd lost all track of Pepe's one remaining aunt.

Then she looked for the photo taken when they said goodbye eight years ago where they all looked haggard and were smiling because they were returning to Cuba. On the back they had all scribbled their names, addresses and phone numbers.

She started with the first one on the list, and dialed.

"Please, I'd like to speak to Dr. Llanes."

"Which one?"

"How many are there?"

"Which one do you want?"

"Who am I speaking to?"

"And who is this?"

"Is Llanes there, or isn't he?"

"Which one did you say you wanted?"

"I'd like to speak to Llanes; there's only one."

"Well that one isn't here. And he's not coming back."

She found a taxi at the corner and she gave the driver the address of the second on the list: East Havana, Building 10, across from the Naval Yard. Some children who were playing out in front told her that Dr. Casanovas sold pumpkins and squash in the Unique Market, but that they could take her to Carballo's house where she could buy bananas cheaper.

She got back into the same taxi and asked to be dropped off at the Market. Along the way, worried about the fare adding up, she made sure the driver got a good look at her thighs. The market was full of fat vendors in undershirts and no one knew who doctor Casanovas was. They sent her from one stall to another, to ask about him. The one selling garlic was named Luis Alberto and he suggested that she go see the engineer Miguelez, over with the *malangas* and other root vegetables. He sent her on to the butcher Acosta, who'd been around there longer than anyone. Acosta, waving his hands to chase off the flies, asked what kind of doctor Casanovas was. Orthopedist, she said, and no, I don't know him, he said.

"Go ask Carballo, who also lives across from the Naval Yard."

"The one who sells bananas?" she asked.

"Used to sell, now he's hooked up with a pizza business."

At the market exit, a crowd of drivers jostled her, offering to take her to Sagua la Grande, Victoria de las Tunas, Consolación del Norte, or San Antonio de Río Blanco. "And now what?" said the voice of the driver who'd brought her from Vedado to the Naval Yard and from there to downtown Havana.

‑   "Get me out of here, now. Take the Malecón route, please."
She looked at the photo and picked out Pablo Vivar on I Street,
456, between 21st and 23rd.

"I'll treat you to an ice cream," she promised the driver as she
got out.

"I'd rather have pizza," he said, "and make it Carballo's."

The door opened and Delia Lage invited her in. She was wear‑
ing a chain around her neck with her first name and first surname
on it.

"What about your second surname?" she asked.

"There is no second one. What do you want?"

"I'm looking for the third one in this photo."

"The third surname in a photo?"

"No, the third man."

"The film?"

"No, it's already printed. Just look at the paper."

"I don't have my glasses on."

"His name was Pablo Vivar and he was an ophthalmologist."

"He was? Why the past tense?"

"Pablo lived here and he worked for a while. He's gone now."

She said goodbye, thinking that they'd both been speaking in
the past tense. The taxi driver was waiting for her, chewing on a
candy and he welcomed her back with a smile, offering her a piece.

"What flavor is it?" she asked him.

"Sweet potato, Miss. Tell me where we're going now."

"Let's try the fourth."

"The fourth?"

"The fourth man in the photo. On 37th between Oeste and
30th, going out Almendares. And call me by my first name,
please."

"And Carballo's pizza?" he asked as she headed up the stairs.
On the door of apartment 4 a notice had been taped, with faded
letters: I'M IN SANTA FE. THE POLE.

When she got back to the street, no one was waiting for her. She
felt bad that she hadn't paid the taxi driver, and relief because she
didn't know how much it would have been.

Eduardo Avilés was the fifth, with an address on San Augustín. She thought about how she would get to the west side of the city while she had something cold to drink across the street from the Pole's.

"It's cherry flavored," said the girl with blotchy skin who was running the stand.

"And it tastes like Benadryl," she answered. "Do any of the buses that run by here go all the way to San Augustín?"

"I don't know, but that taxi driver is waving at you—do you know him?"

"I went over to see the Almendares. Did I keep you waiting long? Did you find your friend?"

"No, to both. How was the river?"

"What river? It's an infamous trickle. I went because my cousin Tamara works over there and she told me they were going to improve it."

"Oh yes? How?"

"Improving the ecosystem. Don't ask me. Get in and tell me where we're going."

"To San Agustín and 23rd Avenue. What did you say your name is?"

"I didn't say. Daniel. And yours?"

"María. How old are you?"

"I'm thirty-four and you're thirty-six. I have one daughter and you've got two boys. Right?"

"Yes. And I get my periods on the fifth of the month. How did you find out all that?"

"Every time you open your purse to look at the addresses on the photo, I see a picture of two boys in your wallet. I guessed at your age."

"Ah. And did you also notice how little money I have?"

"No. I'd like to think you have a lot, because this is adding up, María. Here we are. I'll wait here."

A fat man in an undershirt opened the battered door. "Eduardito? Who remembers him any more? He's been in Miami for five years now."

"With all the shit he used to spout?"

"What's that?"

"I'll treat you to an ice cream, Daniel. You choose the place."

"No, I'd rather get this nightmare over with. Did you find the one you wanted?"

"No. Let's go over to Alamar; I have to find Raimundo Pico de Oro."

"Wait, María. I thought this city was adolescent, but it's not the city, it's you women who improvise too much. How you can think we can go from the north to the east, then to the west, and then back east again? Give me all the addresses and I'll organize them by areas, and cover up your legs because you have to pay me anyway."

"Okay, here's one in Marianao, all right? Avenue 11, number 6404. And I'm not showing off anything, I'm just feeling the heat."

"Who are we looking for there?"

"For Tania Albicans. And don't use the plural pronoun. You can wait for me outside."

"Tania got divorced from my son and she went to Holguín which she probably never should have left. It's on the other side of Holguín, actually. A dumpy little town named Santa Lucia. Do you want a drink of water? You look so tired. Oh wait, you're not pregnant by my son, are you?"

"How many are left besides Raimundo Pico de Oro?"

"Just Jorge Cruz, but he's in Matanzas and you won't want to go there."

"I'll take you up on the ice cream and a pizza, too. Carballo's or anybody else's."

"When we get to Alamar we'll eat and then we'll go on."

"See if you can entertain me on the way. This is more boring than the *Granma* editorials."

"How old is your daughter?"

"Seven. And she wears orthopedic boots. Don't laugh, I spent an entire day talking her into putting them on."

"What did you tell her?"

"That Snow White had worn them."

"And what did she say to that?"

"That she was more like Batman than like Snow White."

"And what did you say?"

"That it wasn't Snow White, but Sleeping Beauty."

"And what did she say?"

"That if she didn't have to wear them when she slept, there was no point in looking like Sleeping Beauty."

"And what did you say?"

"That Little Red Riding Hood had crossed the forest wearing boots like this and before you ask me, she said that she would put them on because she wanted to look like the hunter. You're laughing? I thought I was the one who wanted to be entertained."

"Okay. I'll make you laugh, but later. We're in Alamar already. Can we wait to eat until Matanzas?" she asked while she went running in to ask about Raimundo in building A-54 of Zone One.

A large black man said that was his name.

"No, it's not you. I'm looking for a blond guy about five feet tall."

"Pico de Oro? It won't surprise you, Miss, that with that voice of his, he became a singer in the Cubazul Trio and they're on tour off in Burundi. I'm watching his room for him because I'm very fond of him. See this scar? He saved my life four years ago. You're going already? So soon?"

"Off to Matanzas? That'll be the last stop, Daniel. I'll pay for your pizza and ice cream."

"All right, but let me see those legs again and tell me who we're looking for."

"For Jorge, I told you already, but I don't have an exact address. Here it says a block from the juice stand. There can't be many in Matanzas, can there?"

"Okay. But tell me why we've spent an entire day driving around in circles."

"I'm tired, Daniel. When we get to the Bacunayagua bridge,

we'll stop and I'll tell you about it. All right?"

"And my pizza?"

"When we get there. And ice cream and a beer. I'll even give you a kiss."

"Nothing more?" he asked.

"Nothing more," she answered.

"I don't believe you," he said.

"You'll see," she said.

"There aren't any pizzas," said the waiter. "The ice cream is all gone and the beer is warm."

"Then we'll go on," said Daniel.

"Are you crazy?" asked María.

"Let's climb up to the lookout spot," they both said.

"Begin," he said. "Who are you looking for and why?"

"Why is easy, and who for is easy, too. What's harder is what for."

"I don't understand."

"First tell me what you're thinking."

"That you're lovely. That's my why."

"No, I mean about what I'm looking for."

"You, I don't know. I know what I'm looking for. What's harder is how."

"Daniel, don't tease. It's getting late."

"Good. I've never known if what we see from here is Havana or Matanzas, and when night falls, it won't make any difference. Night doesn't belong to anybody."

"For a taxi driver, you express yourself well. Who are you?"

"And you, who are you, María, saying you don't have time and then squandering it running around."

"We should go back to the beginning."

"Across from the Naval Yard?"

"No, the beginning of the questions. I'm looking for someone who can give me an address in Spain."

"Any old address? I could give you one for Joaquín Sabina, the singer."

"As I was telling you, the address in Spain of someone who was a good friend of mine. And I won't tell you any more. It's your turn. Who are you?"

"A guy. A person. I came back twelve years ago, maybe like you did. I don't want to talk about it. I don't want to remember, María."

"Me neither. I'm looking up all of us who were together then, because someone must know something."

"When were you there?"

"I came back eight years ago, and I was there for two."

"What for?"

"Why'd I go?"

"No, why are you looking for your friend?"

"I'm not sure any longer. Maybe everyone's like you."

"Taxi drivers?"

"People who don't want to remember, who are out of fashion, out of step with others."

"Yeah. Like these mountains."

"Like now, it's night now. And we don't even know who we are."

"Make me laugh, María. Tell me a story."

"Let's look out over the bridge, Daniel. I'll tell you a secret."

"I can guess. That you don't have anything to pay me with."

"No, something else. I don't want to look for Pepe any longer. I don't want to find him."

"And what do you want?"

"I don't know. We're caught in the middle and we don't have anything. Not secrets, not desires, not even this night that you say doesn't belong to anyone."

"And what does that matter, María? If so many nights over there seemed disconnected, what does it matter if this one is?"

"That's true. Like us, like almost everyone. You choose, Daniel, where shall we go now?"

Translated by Mary G. Berg.

The Seventh Thunderbolt

Nancy Alonso

Will any trace remain? So frequently posed and ever unanswered, that question came to mind once again. I thought I'd caught a glimpse of Andrés among the men who, with water up to their chests and still near the craggy coast, were pushing out against the powerful surf a small raft made of planks tied with ropes to inner tubes and topped with a makeshift yellow canvas sail. Four lengths of wood served as improvised oars for the impossible vessel. Every bit as impossible as the notion of Andrés turned *balsero*. No. Not Andrés.

No, Andrés, I can no longer have a child with you, I had said fifteen years ago when I rejected his belated proposition for the first time. Not one to give up easily, he adamantly kept on trying to persuade me with a thousand and one reasons, and always ended by asking me, or himself, the same question, "Will any trace remain?"

I had to overcome first my bewilderment and then my embarrassment in front of the crowd: relatives walking to the very edge with those who were throwing themselves in, needless to explain that in *balsero*-speak this meant leaving by way of the sea; curious residents of the Havana coastline who, just like me, gathered at the shore to see what was happening, among them perhaps the would-be protagonists of the next episode in a remarkable exodus. When I finally decided to call out, "Andrés!" it was too late: the five men aboard the flimsy craft, as the press liked to call them, were screaming their goodbyes, maybe as a way to jack up their spirits for their voyage north toward the Florida beaches, those ninety miles infamously known as "the corridor of death," or toward death itself.

One never knows when a casual decision will change the course of life. The evening I accepted Tere Puerta's invitation—"C'mon, Charito, get out of bed and come to the theater"— did not seem to offer anything out of the ordinary. I was unaware that, somewhere in Havana, that October evening—how many Octobers have passed since then, dear Lord, twenty six of them—a medical student either out of interest or sheer boredom, I never asked, there were so many things I never asked him, was innocently heading to the unplanned encounter not entered into any agenda. That's how Andrés and I met, it was that simple, or rather, we thought we were just getting to know each other then: some social chit chat at the end of the performance as we happened to walk out together, the exchange of names, addresses, the promise to meet again soon, a handshake, goodbyes.

Seeing the *balseros* off had been slowly turning into an arresting spectacle: a woman wept with rage at the possible demise of someone, undoubtedly a loved one—"Don't you see that you're all going to be fodder for sharks?"— another, overcome with horror, followed with her eyes the restless pacing of her son by the water,— "He wants to leave and I don't, but if he goes for it I'm going too"—some young boys helped push out the many rafts, the one with the yellow sail, way ahead of the pack, was easily spotted. What might be going through Andrés' mind at this moment? Is it really Andrés? There were others: a few protected the *balseros* against pirates who'd force their way aboard a raft at knife-point and unscrupulously hitch a free ride; a group splashed indolently in the shallow, focused only on the drag of the undertow—"Get out of there, you're in the way"—some amateur sailors discussed the requisites for a flawless journey,—"they should all tie themselves together first and then to the raft, no way, man, if a wave flips them over, they'd be trapped underneath, yeah, but if the raft gets away from them it's all over, it's better and less exhausting to push out at dusk, you gotta be kidding, no one can find the way in the dark, you guys are insane to go, things are not that bad in Cuba, you're the crazy ones for staying"—Will any trace remain? Andrés was leaving without ever getting an answer, while I held firm to my decision to stay here come hell or high water, on our green alligator-shaped island, our homeland.

It was Andrés' green eyes, as passionate as his words, that slowly undermined my defenses, assuaged my worries, obliterated my misgivings. I barely noticed the change until I was shocked by the anguish of a separation brought about by one or another of the myriad obligations we had at that time —promoting a program of social reforms that we had embraced without hesitation—and by the eagerness to meet again. And then the startling telegram. "For me?"

"Yes, it's for you, Charito, with the most beautiful message." Today the sun turns nineteen years old, signed Andrés.

The sun, a reddish disc floating on the horizon, hastened toward a dawn that was not ours as the yellow sail started to intermittently disappear behind the waves. Much as I tried I could not spot any of Andrés' relatives in the crowd, that's so silly, who knows who his family is these days, his parents might even be dead by now, and as for Angela, the grandmother, no chance that her frail body could still be dragging all her years around. No one budged from their observation posts but the loud chatter was replaced by barely audible whispers when the storm broke out and the sea got progressively more violent. Then lightning, thunder, one, two, three I counted mechanically, four, five, six, please make it stop, seven's a bad omen. And then a rumble, the seventh thunderbolt. The spectators fused into a single emotion: *let nothing happen to them, just let them get there, or back again, either way but safe and sound.* Suddenly and spontaneously we all kept silent. No, that's not right, you don't keep silence, silence is only the void that remains when one tries to hide despair, it is the private face of pain, or as I once heard Andrés quote José Martí, the acceptance of impotence. You don't keep silence, but when it's broken it cracks into pieces, like when a brown dog started to bark—or was he howling?—pointing his snout north, toward one of the many distant rafts, unable to understand, poor beast, he doesn't understand and neither do I, why his master did not take him along this time.

Andrés confided in me one day, with shamefaced amusement, the terror he'd experienced as a child when faced with the dog that always lurked at the end of a dark hallway, the unavoidable entry into Aunt Rosita's apartment house. She was a spinster who lived alone and the family felt obliged to visit on Sundays. Little Andrés had to walk through what, in those days, seemed to him an endless corridor leading to an interior courtyard, the door to Aunt Rosita's apartment was the third one, and he had wished he could fly in order to avoid that path, guarded as it was by a dog very much attuned to his ancestral duties. Hearing his story I remembered, and told him, a similar situation in my own childhood, the main difference being that while Andrés suffered the panic only once a week, for me it was a daily nightmare. I shared an apartment house with a similar dog and I always ended up rushing for comfort to my rocking horse, flanked by two boy dolls turned imaginary defenders. Laughing—how easy to mock long gone fears—we continued adding details of our childish tricks to avoid encounters with the dog. "Ali, he was called."

"Really, so was mine. He was Elvira's dog."

"Elvira, the dressmaker?"

"Yes."

"The widow?"

"Yes, yes, that's the one."

"Then you're Andresito, Rosita the spinster's nephew,"

"And you are Charito, the girl with the rocking horse, forever playing with her dolls."

"Yes, I treasured, and always will, two small porcelain boy dolls with moveable heads and extremities: Andresito 1 and Andresito 2, the Andresitos."

"Why did you repeat the name, Charito?"

Andresito and I were going steady, we were going to get married when we grew up and would have lots of children. It was the best reminder of my first love, twice shipwrecked: first when Rosita the spinster moved unexpectedly, and later due to sheer incompatibility, the details of which my memory, the good kind that protects from accumulated pain and resentment, has allowed me to forget.

The possibility of his being shipwrecked was unbearable. I could no longer make out the raft with the yellow sail, it moved swiftly. I refused to accept such an absurd death for someone like Andrés, who loved life so much he'd take such risks to alleviate his suffering. It hurt to think that, even if they were to make it safely across to the other shore, they would still be shipwrecked: one does not grow roots in foreign soil, where climate, food and language—let alone other so-called old-fashioned values—are all unfamiliar. In any case, they would be condemned to suffer permanent nostalgia. The futility of continuing to search for the ghost of a yellow sail on the horizon soon became apparent: it had vanished. Andrés, however, had never entirely vanished from my life. "They're lucky the south wind is blowing, it happens only every four years, perhaps it's because of El Niño which also comes every four years."

After our breakup Andrés would periodically pop back into my life in unpredictable cycles, but always determined to rescue us from our separateness. Once he looked me up to tell me, just like that, with nary a preamble as if four years had not passed since the last time we had seen each other, that he wanted me to share his life. "Marry me, Charito."

"I can't believe you are asking me that, you so outspokenly independent, so afraid of ties."

I did not explain, indeed I kept from him, the fact that I loved another, I spoke only and not untruthfully, about my fear of one more failure, "Let's not ruin what we have, Andrés." Years later he knocked on my door again, "How did you find me?" "If you seek, you shall find," and showing me the picture of his son he lamented that he was not ours. Later still, one more devastating encounter: his wife had left for the United States taking the child. "Why did you let her do that?"

"She wanted to go, she's his mother and is ill."

"You've lost your only child."

But that was not all, he had lost even more: for having allowed his son to leave he was harassed, forced to ask for permission to leave himself. Out with the scum. "I never wanted to leave, Charito, I swear," though I raged at such intolerance. He lost his job, his only option a transfer to some remote medical outpost to wait indefinitely for the exit visa, many of his friends shunned him. "Please don't you do that, Charito."

"I can forgive you anything, Andrés, your weakness, your arrogance, your hopelessness, but not that you let him go far from your arms," and together we wept for the loss of a child who should have been ours, and also for the one we never had.

I wept that night as the south wind blew, pushing Andrés away —was it indeed Andrés?—perhaps forever away from my life. The question lingered: Will any trace remain? Later I found out that most of the neighbors had not slept either, too many heart-wrenching emotions: the euphoria, the desperation, the daring, the defiance, the recklessness, the naiveté of the ones leaving, each one of them brave in a special way, you have to admire their nerve, their sheer boldness, what a pointless waste of courage. Dawn brought an astonishing piece of news: they were being denied entry into Florida. "I heard it on the radio last night, Charito, they're being sent to the American base in Guantánamo, they won't be given political asylum, they'll be treated just like those wetbacks who cross the Rio Bravo, as undesirables, excludables." Andrés would not be reunited with his son.

Ten years earlier he had resigned himself, not without grief, to the separation. "My place is here, Charito." It was then that he suggested for the last time that we have a child.

"How can I be sure, Andrés, that you will not abandon ours for the other one?"

"No, Charito, this will be the most cherished and lovingly nurtured child."

"Don't fool yourself, Andrés, we are not the same ones we once were; what's left is just a memory," and again the phrase, Will any trace remain? pounding in my head, just like the image of the yellow sail swallowed by the waves.

The news reverberated through the neighborhood: the yellow-sail raft is coming back, the one that left yesterday afternoon, there was some mishap, it's almost here. I don't even know how I made my way to the shore. I felt the water around my ankles, I wondered what the story was, how many were coming back, the distance to the raft seemed insurmountable, the water now up to my thighs, I hope nothing awful has happened, this was no longer the sea that separated me from Andrés, all five were there, the water at my waist, hard to make out their faces, clear the way, let them come in, the sea was reuniting us, so close now, the water chest high: "Andrés!" Abruptly I came face to face with a pair of exhausted brown eyes, back from an unfathomable hell, that stared blankly at me, baffled by my screams, by my tears. "Forgive me."

And finally I had an answer for the question: Yes, there will be traces because I am going to write our story.

Translated by Cristina de la Torre.

Thou Shalt Not Deviate

Nancy Alonso

After talking on the phone with Orestes, Raquel took a bath of the kind that she labeled "spring cleaning," referring to the meticulous scrubbing that people in northern latitudes do to bid farewell to winter and to welcome the first hint of green on the trees. Once in her bedroom she stood in front of the closet and perused her deplorable wardrobe. She glanced at the skirts, mended due to her chronic smoking habit, the faded slacks, the outdated blouses. It was not easy to find something worthy of the occasion. She finally settled on a sky-blue dress with a round neckline that Orestes had given her on some wedding anniversary, who knows how many years ago.

Orestes noticed something odd in Raquel's voice when they talked, and he asked if she was feeling all right. Raquel's reply was so unconvincing that it only succeeded in feeding his growing alarm. No one knew better than he the precariousness of his wife's condition. He felt incapable of helping her out of the hole where she found herself after so many recent calamities. Raquel was hurting, like someone who has a tooth pulled without anesthesia. The

Polish film of that title, *Without Anesthesia,* about a man whose world suddenly falls apart came to mind. He recalled the horrifying ending. No, Raquel would never do such a crazy thing. Yet something inside him kept saying yes, it was possible, so he ran out of his office without stopping to offer any explanations.

Raquel studied herself in the mirror, which showed a body so thin that it made one wonder if that dress had ever belonged to her. Her face was pale and drawn, much too wrinkled for her forty-five years, and her eyes had long ago lost any shine. She made herself up with utmost care, did her hair, put on perfume. She looked better; at least now there was some color on her cheeks and lips. Finally she took her government identification card out of her wallet and put it on the dresser in plain view, hoping to make things easier for the family. She took off her rings and her earrings and placed them in the porcelain box where she kept her valuables.

Orestes rushed out to the street in search of some form of transportation that would take him swiftly to Raquel. His anguish increased when he could not find a taxi, and there was no traffic official around who could have forced any vehicle to stop and take him. Home was more than seven miles away so he gave up on the absurd notion of walking. He stood at the end of the long line and braced himself for the interminable wait, since only a handful of people—as many as got off at any particular stop—could get on the packed buses.

Sitting on the edge of the bed Raquel began searching the bottom of her nightstand drawer. Under a pile of useless items she found the gun. It was the Browning that had been Orestes' constant companion during his days in the underground and then in the army. Raquel stared at it enthralled, not yet daring to touch it. Its silver gleam and clean lines had always held a magnetic fascination for her, the seduction of knowing that all she had to do was take it and turn it into part of her body to make herself powerful. Softly, almost the way one caresses a sleeping child, the tips of her fingers grazed the gun's cold surface, suffusing it with the warmth that emanated from her body. Only then did she wrap her hand around its grip.

It was really difficult to get around Havana at noon, since that was when the bus drivers ate lunch. In the line there was talk that it could well be two hours before any buses came. Frantic, Orestes tried to call home from the corner phone booth. He thought that if he could only get through to Raquel and let her know he was on his way, he would calm down. He reached for the handset and, finding it almost weightless, understood that only the shell remained. He went back to the bus stop feeling defeated, reproaching himself for not having gotten rid of the gun. When he was discharged from the army Orestes had been allowed to keep it as a token of so many years of armed struggle. It had great sentimental value for him since one of his closest buddies, killed at the end of the war, had given it to him. Now Orestes hated the Browning, and himself, for not having anticipated the possibility of a tragedy.

Growing more self-assured with each passing minute, Raquel rummaged through the drawer using the barrel of the gun to push things around until she found the clip. With a swift gesture she slipped it, and the six bullets it contained, into the grip. The gun was now ready to obey her commands. Raquel knew that it could be very simple: lift the barrel to her temple keeping it as level as possible, and pull the trigger with her index finger. The difficult part had been deciding to do it, but that was already in the past. The only thing now was to keep the hand holding the Browning steady, not to hesitate at the end. Just thinking about it made her heart thump. Had Violeta Parra composed that heretical song, Curses, to block any other way out for herself?

After another failed attempt to reach Raquel—this time from a nearby bookstore, but no one answered—Orestes decided to forego any more tries. He would just wait at the stop until the bus eventually came. He decided to have a talk with the children that evening. Together they would find the way to help Raquel out of her pain. Mauricio had dropped out of school despite his parents' objections. He'd argued that not everyone needed a college degree, that someone had to do life's menial jobs: sweep the streets, bury the dead. Faced with what he deemed Mauricio's lack of passion, his weariness, Orestes wondered where they had failed in bringing up their kids. Sonia, the eldest, was very introverted and spent her spare time in church, an inclination that she certainly had not picked up from them. Orestes recalled how, when the kids were little and they had to leave them in the care of others—to attend evening meetings or do time helping with the harvest in the countryside, or when Orestes had been sent to Africa for two years and Raquel had to deal alone with the boy's asthma attacks and the girl's meningitis—he had more than once questioned if they were doing the right thing, or if they were neglecting their own and spending their energies on everyone else's kids, on the children of their children, the ones not yet born. And even though he and Raquel had consoled themselves thinking that it was just a generational thing—it had been like this for parents and children since the beginning of time—Orestes was aware, while Raquel refused to accept it, that something else was going on, something much deeper. The children were angry, resentful of all humankind, beginning with their parents. Yes, the talk could not wait, he had to see them that very night.

The phone rang and Raquel did not react. She remembered the description of Marilyn Monroe's death, the limp body, the arm reaching for the phone. Maybe it was wrong to assume that Marilyn had tried to call for help and, in fact, what she had tried to do was answer someone's call. Raquel decided not to answer. Let God answer, if He existed. She was about to face, of her own accord, the loneliest act that has ever been undertaken by a human being. She thought of the line: "Dear God, how lonely are the dead!" Nothing and no one can offer solace or company to a person about to die and least of all, she well knew, in the case of a suicide. Judged an act of madness by some, of cowardice by others, there are also those who take suicide to be a heroic deed reserved for a select few, those able to lucidly face without flinching the only end they deem dignified. No human act has ever been classified in such disparate terms. Nevertheless, during those moments, Raquel was not considering arguments that could dissuade her from pulling the trigger. She was eager to go ahead with it, certain as she was of the non-existence of an antidote for desperation. It mattered little whether others thought her feeble or daring.

Five people got off the first bus that came, and five got on, which gave Orestes hope that the line might move quickly if this ratio was kept up and the buses rolled on. The comments of some people in the line—the usual pessimists who loved to see it rain on a parade were saying that this might be the only bus running and they might well have to wait for it to come back around—brought him back to reality with a thud. Raquel's problems, in fact, had begun with her refusal to face reality only to run smack into it later, head on. The domestic quarrels caused by her selective blindness had been getting more and more heated. She just did not accept phrases such as deterioration of values, lack of honesty, self-interest. Orestes thought back to the time when she accused him, and especially the children, of giving weight to rumors, of believing slanderous lies. Her own response was to get lost in her work and in the leadership of the union, demanding more of herself and of others. No one could persuade her that this was more than a bad break from which they would recover through their selfless efforts and their commitment. And Orestes would never forget that Raquel remained unconvinced right up to the day when she discovered that the manager of the company where she worked— the same one who had so often called meetings to chastise those who took home the scraps from the cafeteria, the same one that Raquel had so vehemently backed in the firing of two swindlers who were dishonoring the team—was found to be using resources for his personal gain. Orestes could find no words to comfort Raquel, who felt stupid and pathetic for having trusted, and impotent for not having enough evidence to turn her boss in. Orestes agreed with Raquel that the only thing to do was to resign her position in the union and wage a pitiless war against the manager-turned-embezzler. Orestes had not anticipated the consequences of the face-off: the tension at work, the intrigues, the reprisals for insubordination, Raquel's depression. Until one fine day—or rather an awful one—lacking the strength to go on, Raquel quit. Orestes would never forgive himself for having gone along with this decision.

Raquel lay down on the bed determined to get it over with once and for all: there would be no more times for her, like there had been no more poems for Alfonsina Storni. When she put the barrel to her head she experienced what she'd so often read about: her whole life flashing before her eyes. Except not in an orderly sequence but rather as a holograph containing, in glittering detail, all the events of her existence linked together, from the dewdrop on a leaf that she had admired one morning when she was little, to her childish fear of the dark, to the cry of her firstborn, to the day she walked out of her job. Raquel observed the scene, amazed at the wealth of detail in that synthesis.

Once on the bus Orestes' anguish began to subside. He berated himself over and over for not having insisted that Raquel find another job to get her out of the house and help with her depression. After such a long time playing ostrich, interpreting what was going on around her from the same narrow and dogmatic perspective, Raquel had caught a glimpse of a world of unspeakable ethical lapses and injustices previously unknown to her. She opted to hide in the past in order to survive the present. Orestes had witnessed the changes that Raquel had undergone.

With the gun tightly held, Raquel continued surveying the images. There she was working for the betterment of her fellow human beings, burdened since childhood by the social repercussions of her acts. And deep in her essential being she found the ultimate reason for her decision: she had always been convinced of the messianic purpose of her existence, of her power to inspire others to grow and challenge them daily to do so, and her own example was the best way to lead. What was left, now that the blind faith that had guided her destiny was gone? No one would be able to persuade her that not all was lost, as no one would have been able to keep Virginia Woolf from immersing herself in the waters of the River Ouse. With her death Raquel would prevent the bad seed of disbelief from germinating, she would conjure others' despair not with her actions in life but with its end.

When he got off the bus Orestes ran the four blocks to his home. He was utterly desperate to get to Raquel and just hold her.

He could not get the ending of that film out of his mind, or the look on Raquel's face the day Mauricio got into trouble. Orestes could not honestly say that they had been harassed at the police station where he went with Raquel to clarify their son's situation. However, it did seem eerie to him when they were called by the loaded word "citizens," since neither they nor their son were law-breakers, even though he stood accused of driving an illegal taxi. He had been arrested at the airport while renting Orestes' car to some foreign visitors. The young man had no permit to drive a taxi and that kind of activity was strictly forbidden in tourist zones. He was fined fifteen hundred pesos and let go with the warning that, if there were a next time, they would impound the car and throw him in jail. Orestes and Raquel did not defend themselves against the accusation hurled at them by the official in charge: namely, that of neglecting their twenty-year-old son. They already felt guilty enough without going into explanations. The family had decided—after endless discussions and not without bit-terness on Raquel's part—that in order to avoid starvation Mauricio should try to bring home some dollars that way. Since Raquel had stopped working they had only Orestes' salary, which was not enough to feed four people and cover the basic expenses. Sonia was still in school, and Mauricio had not yet found a steady job since dropping out. He was not even good at driving the pirate taxi. Mauricio was simply not very street-wise; he lacked both ambition and savvy. He befriended people and then was embar-rassed to charge them, like those poor Cubans that he took home from the airport when they returned from Uruguay after they told him how touching that country's solidarity had been, and all the medicines its government had donated to Cuba. Orestes recalled how, when Mauricio was freed at the station, Raquel put her arms around her son and burst into tears. The youth looked defiantly at the official and said to his parents: "Let's get out of here." When he reached the door he added, this time addressing the policemen: "And just for your information, I am this poor man's son, I am not some pretty pampered boy, 'cause if I were I would have no need to try to make a living with that rattling piece of tin."

Orestes had never seen such passion in Mauricio and he felt very proud. But for Raquel this episode was the final blow. Orestes could tell that she was touching bottom, so his worry was not unfounded when he noticed the odd edge to her voice over the phone. Orestes reached his house and nervously opened the door.

Raquel pulled the trigger. And in that briefest of instants between the motion of her finger and the sound that she could barely hear, Raquel had enough time to feel the dread of imagining how many more shots like that one she would unleash with her death.

Translated by Cristina de la Torre.

Little Heart

Aida Bahr

I wanted him to look at me that way, like I was the center of the world, like I was all that made life worthwhile. I spent years dreaming of that look, imagining the moment when we'd be face to face and he'd lock eyes with me and slowly smile. That was enough to make my legs go so wobbly I'd be about to fall over. Just imagining it, I mean. I didn't even dream of him kissing me, because I'd have to feel that on my lips and I've never been able to manage it. I can close my eyes and imagine most anything, like I was watching a movie or one of those soap operas on TV that make me go goosebumps all over, but I can't hear any words or feel myself being touched. It must be because I'm dumb. All I finished was ninth grade and that was in the country, and the teachers there are the ones who can't go anywhere else. It's my father's fault, for coming to get us when my mother died. You could say it's my mother's fault, but that's nonsense because, poor thing, how could she want to die, not after fetching my sister and me out of the sticks and bringing us here in search of some development. The problem was just that she died, and my father came running after us. Irene had already turned seventeen. She told him there was nothing for her back in San Carlos. He got real mad, said that Irene was going bad and if that was the path she wanted to take then she wasn't his daughter any more. Since I was only twelve there wasn't anything I could do but go with him—crying the whole way, which only made him worse, so every ten or fifteen minutes he'd haul off and give me a knock on the head to get me to shut up. Luckily it's not that far to go, or else I might have had a stroke from all that banging. He thought I was crying about my mama and Irene, but the truth is I was crying for Luis Angel. For my mama too, but most of all for Luis Angel, and then from the banging on my head. Leaving Holguín meant I wouldn't see Luis again and that was the worst, because I'd been crazy about him for so long, ever since that afternoon in the river. The six years I spent in San Carlos, I always had his face in my head. I'd see him come along on horseback, jump the gate, and gallop right up to where I'd be, always with something in my hands that I'd drop when I saw him, but it would fall slowly, in slow motion, while the horse came closer and closer that same way, like on a cloud. He'd bend over, take hold of my waist and lift me up without reining in the horse. He'd sit me on his legs and off we'd go, in each other's arms, all wrapped up in my hair blowing wild in the wind. That was why I refused to cut it, even when it got to be almost impossible to get hold of soap and my father's wife threatened to shave me bald if I came down with lice. I spent all my time dreaming those things, and little by little I was getting so desperate I thought I was going to die. My father thought so, too, seeing how skinny I was, only he thought it was because we weren't eating anything but bananas and yucca. We had to sell the animals, or trade them for shoes and clothes, and even so we looked like the Cuban soldiers who came down from the hills after the Ten Years' War. One day I'd had enough, so I told my father I was going to live with Irene. He shouted plenty, that I was an ingrate and wanted to go bad like her, but what I think is he was glad to see me take off. He didn't even raise his hand to me, and he told his wife to help me pack my things because, if I wanted to go, the sooner the better. When I went out

the gate I heard him yell from the house that I better not come
back, no matter what, because I wasn't his daughter any more. He
could have saved his breath, because the part about not being his
daughter, I could have guessed, and "no matter what" was a joke,
because what could he ever have to offer? I did feel bad leaving my
three brothers and even my stepmother, who's ugly but not a bad
person. But the truth, the real truth, is I was bursting with happiness about seeing Luis Angel again. That idea kept me going the
three weeks that passed before we bumped into each other, even
though in Irene's house I started to miss the bananas and yucca I
used to have. She ate out, someplace, and what she got from the
ration store she either traded or sold. On my second day of going
hungry I asked her what I had to do to eat, and she said, "Hit the
street and fight for it," but my idea of fighting for it isn't the same
as hers. I can't, well, I'm no good at that, so I started nosing
around the neighborhood and found somebody who'd pay me to
wash and iron for them. So that way I took care of myself, and
whatever I made I spent on fritters and peanuts, to see whether by
eating fats I could stop losing so many pounds. It killed me to
think that when I finally ran into Luis Angel he wouldn't be able
to see me because I'd be transparent. Every time I turned a corner
I'd get ready. I'd stop, stick my right leg out a little, forward, and
my hand on my hip, the breeze ruffling my hair that I left loose
on purpose. He'd stand there staring at me, wondering who I
could be, and suddenly he'd smile, come toward me, take me in
his arms and look at me that way, like somebody who's found the
reason he's alive. But no, nothing. Day after day walking his street
and he wasn't anywhere. The thirteenth of August a neighbor
asked me to go with her to the party in the park for Fidel's birthday and I thought of saying no, that's how down I was, but then
I said to myself, maybe he'll be there. It was packed with people,
because they were selling beer and box lunches, and there was
music and even colored lights. When I got tired of being pinched
and hugged, and Lilita ran into some other friends, I told her I
was leaving. Just before I got to the corner of Marti and Maceo I
suddenly saw him, coming the opposite way down the middle of

the street while I was underneath the arcades. My heart started hopping like crazy and I took off, bumping people right and left to try to get close. He was about to go right past without seeing me, with one man still in between. I reached out my arm, desperate, grabbed him by the shoulder and yelled, "Luis Angel!" He looked at me, the other man moved a little, and I squeezed through so we were face to face. More than face to face, but that was the crowd's fault, not because I was pressing myself against him like that gossip Elder told Berta I did. Luis didn't recognize me, not even when I told him my name, but then I mentioned Irene and he remembered. He smiled and asked, "Are you by yourself?" I said I was, and we went on toward the dance. He introduced me to Elder who luckily and discreetly made himself scarce pretty soon, so we spent most of the night alone, dancing very close, and it was good thing the crowd hardly left us any space to move in, because that way he couldn't tell I'd only danced a couple of times and *El pasito de la bibijagua* was all I knew. By real late at night there weren't so many people, but we kept on dancing so close. I watched these bright, colored fireworks floating in the air,and I would have liked them to play a waltz so I could go turning and turning in his arms like the last scene of Disney's *Sleeping Beauty*. He said we'd better go. We walked along with our bodies brushing till we got to the bridge, where he leaned back against the wall and pulled me toward him. We were tight together from our feet to our waists, but above that he kept us a little apart, holding my arms so he could look into my eyes. And that look—like a blanket wrapping me up because I was cold, and it so real I even started to shiver. He said it was amazing I remembered him after so long, and then I made my decision and told him softly that ever since that afternoon at the river I hadn't been able to stop thinking about him. He scrunched his brows together, which is what he does when he doesn't understand something, his eyebrows make almost a Y shape together with his nose. I reminded him that on that afternoon he was with a bunch of other guys and I was following them along the river, to see what they were going to do with old Arnoldo's nanny goat. Two of them spotted me and pushed me way under the water so I almost drowned, but he pulled them off and even got in a fight with them, because didn't they realize I could die from some infection—they call it a river but it's not much more than a sewer in fact. They laughed and wanted to chase me away with stones. He didn't let them. He took me a ways off and said, "You're a girl. Don't go following us any more." It was as if he'd let me in on a big secret to me, something huge that made me feel like crying and strangely happy all at once, the same happiness I've felt every time I've thought of him since. That last part I didn't tell him, I didn't need to, because as I was about to he started to smile, to look at me tenderly, shining the way I'd dreamed about. The world disappeared on me, there was nothing left but the two of us, his face, his lips searching for mine. I closed my eyes but I could see the fireworks exploding in the sky over our heads. I still get goosebumps remembering it. In the next few days we were only apart to wash, eat, and sleep. I mean, he ate, at his house, because the state I was in, I gave up washing clothes and that left me flat broke. Then Irene went to the beach at Guardalavaca with some Italians and left me alone in the house. I fixed it up the best I could, really what I did was fill it with flowers that I stole from all the nearby yards, but it looked very pretty, shiny clean with garlands hiding the cracks and chips in the broken walls and chairs, as long as he didn't try sitting in any of them. It didn't cross my mind, not for an instant, that he might think I was too easy, because I'd spent eight years loving him, eight years waiting for him. When it came time to go to bed I was afraid. He could tell it was my first time and again he looked at me in that beautiful way, as if I were something very precious, very delicate, that he needed to take good care of. He kissed me and told me not to be afraid, that he wouldn't harm me, that he wanted the best for me. I gave myself up to his arms and yes, it hurt, but that was nothing compared to the joy of knowing I was his woman now. The next day Irene came back and saw through everything. She got an ugly look and told me, "You, just like always, screwing up again. That guy has a girlfriend and all he wants to do is laugh at you." I didn't pay her any mind. I'd already convinced myself that none of her old self was left. Of course she was still my sister, but she'd turned into somebody hard, the kind that laugh to see an old person fall down, the kind that if they see somebody else happy, that bothers them. Even the soap operas get this right, there's always one villain who tries to put roadblocks in the paths of the heroes and heroines—and generally there's more than one. That's just what happened with us, only Irene was the first in line and I never would have thought she could do what she did. Even if she didn't like my relationship with Luis, she didn't worry much about it either—she always lived her life without worrying much about mine. But one weekend she went to Las Tunas with some friends and Luis moved in with me, like other times. When I say moved in, that's in a way of speaking. He went back to his house for his bath and he ate there too, because even though I was now doing my little bit of laundry when I needed to, to buy something so I wouldn't die of an empty stomach, there was no way I could provide him with the food he got in his house. It's not for nothing that his father drives a semi and can arrange things so he never comes back from a trip with empty hands. So he'd gone home to his house that Saturday, for a bath and a meal. I had my bath too, and because we were planning to go out I got the bad idea of putting on an outfit of Irene's, because by this time Luis already knew my four rags by heart. I call it a bad idea even though I don't think things would have turned out any different if I'd worn something of my own. She had a problem in Tunas, a serious problem that made her come home ahead of time and turned her into an animal. When she opened the door of the house, I was just coming out of her room, all put together and made up nice, and I practically fainted when I saw her. She looked me up and down, dropped her suitcase on the floor, put her hands on her hips and tossed her head to one side like a bull about to charge. And that was what jumped me, a savage beast. I didn't even defend myself, I was so frozen with fear. She threw me around by my hair, scratched me, yanked off the dress, practically tore it off, all the while beating on me and screaming *Bitch, ingrate, I'm going to kill you, bitch.* I managed to drag myself to the bathroom and lock myself inside. She kicked at the door for a while and then went out on the patio. I heard her yelling to a neighbor that she'd let the enemy into her house, that I was a damn bug, a vermin, a bitch. She said that over and over like that was her way of getting rid of some of her rage. Afterward she calmed down some, came back in, and told me I had five minutes to get my stuff and beat it. "If you're here when I get back, I'm going to make sure they can't put you back together even with a map," she shouted as she left. I rushed to gather up my things and flew out of the house, without even noticing whether anybody in the neighborhood was watching the show. I sat down on the last bench in a little park that's two blocks away, where I kept watch for Luis. I was terrified he'd some-how show up at the house, but luckily I saw him in time and called him over. I could tell from his face how bad I must have looked. Right then I started to ache from every blow and burst out crying like somebody unhinged, and night fell while I was explaining it all to him. He took me right to the hospital, figuring I must have a broken rib at least, and on the way he tried to convince me to file a complaint with the police. I said I'd rather go sleep under a bridge than have to face Irene again. I said, the police aren't going to come live in the house with us. He didn't say any more, not even when his friend who took care of me in the emergency room said, halfway joking, brother, you let yourself get out of control. Afterward, we went walking slowly as far as the Avenida de los Alamos, where he finally decided to ask me, you really don't have anywhere to go? I could see my father's face if I showed up there like this, and I told him no I didn't. His shoulders tightened, he sighed, and he said, let's go to my house. We went in quiet as mice so we wouldn't wake up Berta. Reynaldo, his father, was off on a trip. We took off our clothes and snuggled up in his bed. I fell asleep with my arms around him and I guess I was so tired, had been through so many emotions, and then the sedatives they gave me in the emergency room, all that made me drop into such a sound sleep that I didn't hear a thing when Berta got up and made coffee in the morning or even when she opened the door to come wake Luis with his cup of coffee like she always did. What woke me was her screaming and the cup breaking when it hit the floor. Such a pretty cup, porcelain with cute designs. Luis and I sat up, bolt upright both at once, and there was Berta bent over like some-body had stabbed her in the belly, she had her hands over her eyes so she wouldn't see this horrible sight, because for her it was like seeing the devil to find me there, with my mouth split open, my swollen black eye, and the scratches on my neck all painted with mercurochrome. I understand that, that's why she ran back out of there when Luis reacted and tried to explain, Mama...and she wouldn't listen to him in the kitchen either, she just started yelling Hail Mary Full of Grace, What's going on here, God help me, This can't be real, Oh my God! To top it off, here came Reynaldo who—he said—had just gotten back but had stopped off first to leave the truck at the depot. Ten minutes later along came Marisela, the next door neighbor, and now both of them were yelling too, trying to find out what was going on, so Luis couldn't even make himself heard in the middle of all that racket. Through it all I was still in bed with the sheet over my head wishing the earth would swallow me up, or at least that Luis would think to close the door. Suddenly Reynaldo let loose such a violent shout, like Cut it ouuttt!, that everybody shut up at once, just like on TV. At last Luis got to explain what had happened, but the minute he closed his mouth the whole ruckus broke out all over again. Berta and Marisela were both repeating themselves, but with Berta it was You can't do this, while Marisela was stuck on, You screwed up. That was when Reynaldo asked Luis if he'd thought about what was going to happen when Karina got back from Havana. I uncovered my head and sat up in bed, still wrapped in the sheet. Luis said Karina and he had split up before she left, and anyway he couldn't just leave me to live in the park. "And besides, she's my woman," he concluded. That challenge shut them up, and I decided to get up and close the door so I could dress. When I came out I didn't even dare say good morning. Marisela had dis-appeared, Berta was making breakfast, Reynaldo and Luis were sit-ting at the table—all of them with faces like World War III had just been declared. We ate breakfast in silence and then Luis took me back into his room. He told me he had to go out but he'd be back for lunch. Go help Mama, he told me, and don't argue with her about anything. I went into the kitchen and spent the rest of the morning trying to help Berta, which was kind of uncomfortable since she wouldn't talk to me. When she started cleaning rice I sat down to help her, but right away she stood up and left me to do it by myself. The same thing happened when I tried to peel *boniatos* with her. When I finished with that she was very busy scrubbing the soot off a pot, so I decided to sweep the house on my own. That's how that day went by, and the next one, and the next. The only voice was Marisela's. Since she'd gotten laid off she'd lived on her sixty percent benefit and whatever she could pick up at Luis's house. The men spent the day out of the house, because Luis's classes had started and his father was always away on a trip, so much so that I thought he must be the most dedicated driver of all. When he was home, Luis didn't talk much. He looked worried, except that in bed it only took the slightest touch for him to embrace me with the same passion as before, only now in the darkness I couldn't see his eyes, so instead I'd close mine. Besides imagining his look, I got to pretending we were in a fancy hotel and I was slipping out of a lacy negligee, little by little, as he kissed me. The kisses were real, except sometimes they didn't match up with where they should be according to what was going on in my head. I felt happy and got so used to sleeping with him that when he started having night duty in the hospital I had trouble getting to sleep in spite of having the bed all to myself. That—not being able to get to sleep—was how I found out. The heat was suffocating and I was bored with tossing and turning so I thought I'd go out in the patio to try and cool off. I went very quietly so as not to wake Berta, who was sleeping by herself too. I stood with my arms stretched out to try and catch a little breeze, but what I caught were little laughs that sounded like kids up to some kind of trick. I realized they were coming from Marisela's house, so I climbed up on the washing sink to see what was going on. I peeked over the wall, very cautiously, and there were the two of them: Marisela in her nightgown and Reynaldo in his shorts, chopping open some coconuts with a machete. They'd been drinking, that was evident, and that was why Reynaldo was laughing, I think. Maybe Marisela thought he looked funny, with his bald head and his bare gut and the big boxer shorts hanging over his legs like a skirt. It was funny for me too, I have to admit. I sat down on the sink and listened for a while, but then I felt strange, nauseous, and went back to bed. I didn't say anything to anyone, though I sure wanted to because of the shameless way he showed up at eleven the next the morning, "just back from Guantánamo," with a sack whose contents were shared out with "poor" Marisela, who arrived, as usual, in shorts that showed off her thighs. If only I'd thought about it, from the moment I met her I was sure she was another one of those soap opera villains, a tramp, a snake, not to be trusted. It was Marisela who asked Luis Angel one day on his way to the hospital, "How's Karina doing in her sixth year?" That's how I found out that she was in medical school like him. Now every time he left for classes my heart skipped a beat thinking he was going to be with her. Because of all that, I took pity on Berta. I started to talk to her, to be almost caring and sympathetic with her. She wouldn't answer, just looked at me in a suspicious way that would make you think I was the witch in *Snow White* offering her a bite of apple. So I left her alone, okay, one day she'd find out the truth and she'd see how unfair she'd been. Then she'd have to come to me with her head down and say, "I was wrong about you," and I'd say, "Don't worry about it, Berta, there's nothing to be sorry for," and we'd give each other a hug. Nothing like this happened, but it would have been pretty. Sometimes I imagine things so much I believe them, and then I don't know what really happened. Anyway I started to treat Berta as if we were friends and sometimes in the midst of the housework she'd forget her suspicions and answer me. I was almost on the point of telling her, the day I got terrible cramps and dizziness and almost fell down in the bathroom. I realized I hadn't had my period since I left San Carlos. I was so terrified that my first impulse was to call out to Berta and tell her about it, but I thought it over and decided to keep quiet. I didn't even tell Luis, which mixed things up worse because that

night he started caressing me and I said, "Tonight I can't." I wasn't
trying to fool him, the fact was I really couldn't because I was so
upset, though later I understood he thought it was the other thing.
I wondered what was going to happen when they found out. I tried
to imagine Luis in front of me, smiling, taking my hands and saying, you're making me the happiest man in the world, but for some
reason that scene began to grow dimmer, it got hazy with smoke,
and through the smoke I could just make out his eyes, dark and
serious, the eyes of a man condemned to death. I started to get
crying jags, any little thing made me burst into tears and it was
really hard to stop. One day I was doing my laundry and ripped a
blouse just by giving it a hard scrub—that's how worn the fabric
was—and I broke down sobbing on the spot. I felt horrible remembering the day my stepmother sewed it for me, I don't know, it was
like the way when somebody dies you remember the day they were
born. I was crying so hard I wiped my face with soapy hands that
stung my eyes, my nose was running like a fountain, and even
Berta took fright. She didn't say a word, but to console me she sat
down at the sewing machine and made me a blouse out of an old
dress of hers. That touched me so I started crying again, or at least
the tears came back. I told her how well she sewed, and how quickly,
and she told me that she'd done a lot of sewing to pay for the roof
of the house. In my new blouse I waited up for Luis, but at eleven
I gave up and went to bed, a puddle of tears. I couldn't sleep, I
tossed and turned in bed and by five a.m. I couldn't take it any
more. I got up to make coffee, Berta heard me, and she came into
the kitchen, too. I know she was worried about me, women can't
stay walled off when we see someone suffering, to do that you have
to have a very dark and hardened and insensitive soul. Berta is a
good person, in fact she's too good. Her problem with me was
that she cared a lot for Karina and anyway, who's going to feel
good about exchanging a daughter-in-law who's a doctor, fine and
well-mannered, for a skinny country girl with no place to flop.
Anyway, she came in the kitchen to share the morning chores with
me. Go back to bed, I told her, it's still early. Reynaldo's coming
home today, she told me, I'm going to make him some candied

guava peel. She sat down to work on the guavas. In five minutes she started complaining about the heat and went over to open the window. I was washing the pots from the night before and, even though I had my back to her, I noticed how long she just stood there by the window, and I thought it was strange. When I turned around I saw she was standing stock still, petrified, white as a sheet. Then I realized she was looking over toward Marisela's house. I went to the window and looked: the slats on Marisela's bedroom window were open, and in the bed you could see the bulk of one body and the empty space on the other side; the bathroom light was on where somebody was taking a shower. I pried Berta away from the window and shut it. I helped her sit down and brought her a cup of coffee. Herb tea would have been better, but I didn't have anything at hand. Anyway she didn't drink the coffee. She left it on the table and went to her room. It took her over an hour before she came back. Do you want breakfast, I asked. She shook her head no. She opened the window and looked. Marisela had closed hers by now. Berta turned toward me. How long have you known? I didn't know how to answer her. Don't play dumb, she insisted, you knew it. So I told her. She didn't answer me, just barely nodded like saying yes to herself. Then she shut herself up again in her room. I took care of everything, and when Luis came I forgot all about how he stood me up the night before. I ran to the door to tell him what had gone on, but I couldn't because just then Reynaldo parked his truck in front of the house. I opened my eyes real wide as a signal to Luis, who scrunched his eyebrows together without understanding a thing. Reynaldo called him to help with the usual sack, and they came into the house together. Where's Berta, was the first thing Reynaldo asked. In her room, I said. Is she sick, Luis worried, and right then she opened the door and came out, very determined, with an old suitcase in her hand. What's all this about, Reynaldo asked in the tone of somebody who knows what's coming. Berta held the suitcase in front of her and said, very calmly, Here are your clothes, take them to Marisela's. Luis murmured, Now it's out, so softly that only I heard him, because it was at the same time that Reynaldo was loudly demanding, What do you mean? Get out of this house and go live with that whore, was the sentence Berta pronounced, pointing an accusing finger at Marisela who was coming in with her usual smile but when she heard Berta she turned right around and headed off double-time, so agile that any militia trainer would have given her a commendation. You're crazy, Reynaldo thundered. What I was, was blind, she answered him, but today I saw you, I saw you! Then she shut herself up in the bedroom again. Reynaldo turned toward us, and I, just in case, ran into the kitchen and got ready to serve lunch. Reynaldo paced a few times, up and back, and then he and Luis went knocking at Berta's door, asking her to open it because they had to talk. When she ignored them Reynaldo got upset and yelled that she better not think he was going to leave his own house, after which the two of them sat down to eat with an appetite multiplied by the trouble looming over them. They didn't even look at me. Around two, when Berta didn't come out, Reynaldo said he was taking the truck back to the depot, and he left. Berta came into the kitchen before the sound of the motor died away. I gave her the plate that I had served and covered for her, and she sat down to eat lunch. Luis seized the moment to say, You can't do this to Papa, you don't have anything to complain about with him. Oh, no?, I let slip, and he looked at me with eyes that could have killed. He's always taken care of you, Luis went on, he brings you what you need, he even built this house. And your mother didn't do anything?, I exploded at him. Did the money she earned sewing go to buy herself elegant clothes and fancy shoes? You shut up, he shot back at me, and of course that made me feel so bad I went into the bedroom to cry, sitting on the floor because by now, from all the soakings, the mattress was on the point of rotting away. Whatever else they said, I didn't hear it. I just know Berta wouldn't let herself be convinced, so they had to fix up a bed in the kitchen for her to sleep in the nights Reynaldo spent at home—which were more in a row than there used to be, because he seemed not to have so many trips to make. Marisela took her son and went to some relatives in Puerto Padre. Luis pretty much took off, too. According to what he said, when he didn't have hospital duty and didn't come home, he was at Elder's house. That's how things stood on the fourth or fifth day after the big blow-up, when I was in the kitchen cleaning rice and Berta went to answer the door. I clearly heard her say, Hey, girl! and then, softer, What are you doing here? My heart stopped cold because even before I heard the voice, and even though nobody said any names, I knew who it was. She said, I had to come see you, Luis told me what you're all going through. Berta didn't seem to know what to say, but she delayed asking her to come in and sit down. I slipped out into the patio, came around to the porch, and squatted down underneath the living room window so I could hear them even if they talked very low. They discussed what had happened, with all the usual words: I never expected this from him, after so many years, right here next door, such a lack of respect. Suddenly Karina told her, Don't torture yourself, this is going to pass, Reynaldo knows that woman doesn't measure up to the soles of your shoes. Really, that's the same thing I would have said if Berta had trusted me more. Then Karina went on, Look at me, I've taken all this with Luis very calmly, I know how to protect my place. I stood up like a shot, and I don't know what I would have done if there had been any poles or rocks on the porch. Berta cut her off: Don't make comparisons, you and Luis aren't married and it looked like you'd broken up. Besides this girl isn't so bad, she's just a poor thing who's so in love with Luis Angel, in this case the one who's going to suffer is her. All the strength and anger I'd been feeling drained away with these words. I didn't want to hear any more. I cried a little in the patio, but then I controlled myself. When Berta came in the kitchen, she found me devoted to cleaning rice, though she must have noticed that the pile was still about the same as before. She didn't say anything, so neither did I. From that moment on I knew I had to think about what to do with my life. Sooner or later the bubble would burst and then where would I go, especially now that it wasn't only me? I went through two horrible days thinking about nothing else. I worked and ate like a robot. Since Berta stopped talking to Reynaldo, I'd taken over whatever needed to be done for him, so I didn't have any lack of things to keep me busy, but I couldn't keep my mind on them. The truth is that my brain was like soap suds, every thought seemed to slip away from me halfway through. Berta says she could tell I was in bad shape and so she started keeping watch over me. I didn't notice. I just paid attention to Luis in the moments he was in the house. I spent my time trying to look into his eyes and interpret the tone of his voice. Whatever he said would go on echoing through my head after he was gone. When he came home early one afternoon, I knew something was wrong. He beat around the bush and then finally asked Berta to help him find something or other in the closet. As soon as he got her into the bedroom I put my ear to the bathroom wall so I could hear. Karina wants us to get married in December, he told her. I was about to faint, I broke into a cold sweat and my ears started to hum. I could barely understand when Berta asked him what was the rush, but Luis's answer came through as clear as if the whole world was standing still so I could hear: She says she wants to get pregnant before she graduates so she doesn't have to do her Social Service in the mountains. I felt a strange pain in my ribs, a pain that doubled me over and made it almost impossible to breathe. My eyes clouded over and when I opened them Luis was lifting me up and Berta, very frightened, was saying, Check and see whether she banged her head. Luis carried me to the bed and they rubbed scented alcohol on my forehead. Both of them gave me worried looks. It was nothing, I told them, I banged my hand and went into the bathroom to throw some water on my face. Whenever I bang something hard I'm likely to faint. They didn't seem to believe me but what else could they do? I spent the rest of the day in bed. Berta insisted I take a phenobarbital that night, and really I slept without even dreaming, a deep sleep I had trouble waking up from. It was so late that Luis had already left and Berta had to serve Reynaldo breakfast. I spent the morning straightening and cleaning everything in our room. I got all of my stuff together, nice and neat on one side of the closet. After lunch, Reynaldo left and Berta lay down for a nap. I went to the bathroom and picked up the packets of phenobarbitol. There were twelve pills, which seemed like enough. I took them two at a time. Toward the end I wanted to throw up, but I held on. Before lying down I had time to look everything over. I said goodbye to this place where I'd wanted to live, which was like saying goodbye to Luis Angel. Then I disappeared. Berta says she figured it out when she found the packets in the wastebasket, and luckily Reynaldo came home right then and helped her get me to the hospital. He ran into the emergency room with me in his arms, as if I were his daughter, with Berta crying so everybody thought she must be my mom. It would have been beautiful to see. I just remember a very strong light hurting my eyes and the sensation of falling into a bottomless endless well. Then I remember a terrible dizziness, nausea, and everybody's faces floating in the air. I remember Berta's voice saying, Why didn't you tell us anything? Are you crazy? The scare you threw into us! I remember saying, Luis is going to leave me, he doesn't want this baby, and a voice—maybe Luis?—saying, don't talk nonsense. I don't know whether I dreamed all that. This morning I woke up for real and that intern with the glasses told me what happened to me. I asked to be discharged, but she says not until they get results from today's tests. When everybody came to visit, Berta hugged me and kissed me. Reynaldo patted me on the head. It seems like now they're speaking to each other. Luis sat on the edge of the bed and watched me very seriously the whole time. When it was time to go he told me, We have to talk. And now I really don't know what I'm going to do, because he'll come and offer to give his name to the child and support it, or who knows what, and I don't care about any of that. All I wanted was for him to look at me that way—like I was the center of the world, like I was all that made life worthwhile. There was a time when he did that. Or maybe I invented that look and put it in his eyes, or maybe I saw myself in them, and what I saw was the reflection of my own love.

Translated by Dick Cluster.

Absences

Aida Bahr

Sheets of rain are falling on the patio as before, but the flagstones are paler, not so lustrous, sunk deeper into the ground.
Sheets of rain are falling on the patio and my skin forms goosebumps, for skin has memory. The drops had the force of gunshots
at times, once hail even fell. In the corner, where the eaves meet,
the stream was strong and cold and dirty. The downpour is like a
shadow, a veil in front of the adobe wall and the flowerbed invaded
by the hyacinth which finally took over the spot of the roses and
begonias, and this time no one has put a plug into the drain. The
patio does not turn into a swimming pool this time, the cousins
are not jumping and twirling and splashing, but there in the corner stands the iron pipe that once held up the roof over the laundry sink—the pipe in whose far end lived an indolent green frog,
the pipe you had to run away from when lightning fell, and then
the patio door opened like the door to a helicopter and the children were quickly hoisted away, wrapped in towels, saved from the
volleys of thunder, saved from inundation and disaster. Now
nobody swims in the patio. The children left one day and disap-

peared. Perhaps grandmother's death scared them, or the free boarding schools captured them, or the hurry to live their lives. Maybe they left the afternoon that nobody remembered to collect the toys, which dawn found scattered about the patio like victims of combat, which were hurriedly buried in the wooden chest under the furious voices of the grownups. Now that it's raining the memories return, but not the children. There where you can see the crack in the border of the flower bed, Tito fell and broke open his chin. With a little effort you can see the big drops of blood falling while the rest are screaming, only the rest, because Tito's surprise at his skin hanging down like a torn pocket didn't allow him to feel any pain. Tito is missing, like the large board which served for playing circus when leaned against the wall. A quick race of jumping and climbing, even if it was only a few steps. The dream was to get up there to the top of the wall and see into the neighboring patios. Valdo was the envy of everyone the day he touched the top with his hands, but he slipped. The board was wide and tough; laid across two piles of bricks it supported everyone's weight in the game of jumping and holding the position in which you fell, poses coolly evaluated by a treacherous judge who delayed his verdict until the weakest blinked, or wobbled, or scratched their nose. One day the board broke in two, that could have been the day. Now the board is missing, Tito is missing, as are so many things. The downpour is falling on the patio and everyone sees it with different eyes. Who knows whether Tito, there in the jungle, remembered seeing it fall? He never wrote; perhaps he didn't remember either, but there's a hope, or at least a doubt. With the others, I know, there's no point in asking. They would say yes, but mockingly, with annoyance, which is to say no. To remember is not to know what happened, no, to remember is to be capable of living it again. The flagstones felt rough when you crawled on them, the wall was splashed with the dirt that the water pulled from the flower bed, the iron pipe grew cold as an ice cube and when your thighs pressed against it the feeling was very strange. They don't remember any of this. Valdo can't revive the vertigo of the fall, the sense of being broken in two, of someone turning your lungs inside out and not letting the air back in. He can't feel all over again how they rubbed his back, he doesn't hear the voices saying: he's dead, he's dead; Valdo, does it hurt? Hurry, tell mama, tell auntie, look for ice! Valdo, does it hurt you much? The patio looks lonelier in the downpour. The water complains as it escapes through the drain, it's hurt that no one looks for the rock to stop it up. The drops fall on the stones without sliding over bodies. Now no one thinks of hugging all together and joining their chests to hold up the water and make a little well there so close to their hearts. The sheets of rain call out from the patio, offering their last attempt. Soon the rain will end, and everybody will go on, to resume the dispute over dividing up this house and this patio, to require money in exchange for these worn-out stones, for the portion of the flower bed and hyacinth that's theirs; they've measured the centimeters and divided the ones that Tito can't claim. The rain weeps weakly now in the patio because the children, who loved each other so much, won't ever come back.

Translated by Dick Cluster.

At the Back of the Cemetery

Ena Lucía Portela

The man with the machine sighed. Another trip in vain. How long were those people going to keep this up? Patience.

Standing before him this time was the boy. He couldn't have been twenty, but he looked like a little old man, not just because of his gray, almost white hair but also because of that peculiar, drawn look that really gullible types get in the course of a single night of terror, during a brief descent into the external abyss (anguish) and the internal one (hopelessness).

The man with the machine observed the boy warily. Yes, the kid was a wreck, a sorry mess. Not just his physical appearance, the moralist—which I am not—would have asserted, perhaps to make clear that facts aren't always presented that way, that we accede to the description of a character at his most decadent moment that we assume follows an evil deed.

In any case, he was a wreck, detritus, just short of being a living cadaver. His limbs were weak, not solid at all, yet very heavy at the same time, too leaden for such unusual skinniness, you might say. His nerves were so fragile he trembled at the slightest effort, like the tense tendons of some guy who has been the butt of a very cruel joke and hasn't recovered from it yet. The slightest noise, a creak, a shadow would have frightened him.

His voice, icy and gelatinous as if you could touch it, was a barely audible whisper, so the man with the machine got right up close to hear.

"For the love of God, don't think I'm crazy... But take it away! Take it really far away! If you get it away from me, I'll tell Lavinia you were here again, go on and maybe I can convince her. For the love of God!" He kissed his fingers that formed a cross and the look in his eyes shifted from panic to hope within the panic. "Take it away? OK? Say you will!"

The man with the machine scratched his head...

One fine day, a day like any other, Mama and Papa may have thought enough was enough, they'd had it up to here and took off. Leaving behind the house of half rotten boards at the back of the cemetery; the outskirts; the insidious filth and grime and the cockroaches that grew fat on all the poisons, including those containing D.D.T., M.I.P.C., methyl chloride and a variety of chlorofluorocarbons. In other words, they disappeared off the face of the earth. In unison, nimbly, gracefully, like the best *pas de deux*.

Sometimes they got postcards of snowy landscapes or fall colors from latitudes where there is a fall, or pressed maple leaves and even briefer letters, their postmarks smudged, like those a casual acquaintance who lives at the opposite end of the world might compose as he waited for the train whistle on the platform. One of those types who, before vanishing once and for all into the crowd, send their address, likes and dislikes to magazines with a pen pal section. *How are things going there? Everything's great here. We're doing well. Proud of you both.* And so it went a couple of times a year. Never photographs.

Maybe the Misfortune occurred, something too tragic to be recounted with a chatty smile at sensible people's dinner table. Mama and Papa ill, mutilated, imprisoned or dead, who knows where or why. In any case, a friend, a compassionate soul or even

Lavinia herself (such a good story teller, so full of ways to breathe life into the inanimate, subjugating the totem with all its trappings to the insignificant will of mankind) penned signs of that other life, and constructed a ghostly retreat where nothing ever happened, a hill--or dale--stripped of adventures, of conflicts, nearly of words. *Everything's great here... We're doing just fine...* Set in the limbo of indifference, invented so Lisander could have a care free, happy childhood, in a way as free as Huckleberry Finn.

Naturally they set off together through the cemetery--they chased each other, played, kissed each other in secret and each one letting the other see "down there." Play Town. For them alone. A town with no ambitions beyond the walls, rusty bars and the door to the peace where their bodies and the light itself reduce their sphere of influence to the minimum.

They knew every stone, grave and epitaph by heart. All the alleyways and miniature gardens, the ceiba trees, trumpetwood trees, framboyan trees that cast their shadows on the Shadow. Hand in hand, with a candle stub encrusted in a small candlestick, they'd go down into the crypts, small in comparison to the catacombs and remote labyrinths described in horror stories, e.g., Conan Doyle, H. P. Lovecraft. Out of curiosity they scrambled down there, when the watchman had walked far away, to delve deeper into the dark of the underworld, the old bitter, earthy smells, the phosphorous glow of decaying matter, the will-o-the-wisps and the barely legible inscriptions. The watchman would scold them if he caught them touching each other. At the top of his lungs, he called them rotten brats headed for a children's detention home. That's why they called him "El Brujito, The Little Sorcerer of Burubu."

Ah, the inscriptions! Joe Blow: irreproachable worker, exemplary father and husband. A drunk, Lavinia explained. Mr X: a martyr for the homeland in one of the wars in the last century. An apostate, she'd shoot back, very proud of the word. John Doe: modernist poet who choked once and for all on a mouthful of blood because people with tuberculosis shouldn't laugh so hard. When all is said and done, what are they laughing at HOPE: SVM

QVOD ERIS...

"What's that?" Lisander would ask.

"Sum quod eris..." Lavinia murmured to herself. "Can you believe it? Just a couple of days ago, I looked that up in the pink pages of the Larousse Dictionary."

"So?"

"It says 'What I am, you will be.' It's about you."

"Me? You mean I'll be a skull and skeleton and all that, too?" Lisander would ask, uneasy.

"That's very likely," Lavinia would smile very wickedly.

"And worms'll eat me?"

"That's nearly a sure thing," Lavinia would smile even more wickedly, her face bloodless, pale lips pressed tight and eyes like a hawk's floated in the dark like a lost mask. "You're very tasty."

With great enthusiasm—and unconfessed terror—her little brother shrugged his shoulders. Only a circumstance as menacing as that could draw him out of his habitual, excessive reserve. Along with other contemptuous and obscene tough guy grimaces, he would throw caution to the wind and stick out his extremely long tongue at her, the wet blanket of the graveyard. It looked like the tongue of the little devil who tempted St. Simeon Stylites, the mystic who sat atop a pillar. He did a clumsy, frenetic dance right there, kicking up a huge cloud of dust.

"I don't care! Nana-nana-na-na! I don't care!"

Just then, El Brujito would appear with his flashlight, from behind some bushes. What a scare! He'd grab the boy by the ear, twist it and shake him back and forth before Lavinia could rescue him from the cursing dwarf. Where's the party? What kind of respect for the dead is that, hmmm?

They would hide not only from El Brujito (One day I'm going to pull your heads off! he'd growl and rub the mark on his arm Lavinia's double row of little teeth had left), but also from the cemetery's other nocturnal strollers: love birds; drug addicts; necrophiles; people collecting herbs and the nighttime cults that got together for some sorcery (full moon, end of the Tata Ngana, a small, buried caldron that contained the power of Mt. Izambi when it blows its top in Ecuador); priests of Satanic sects holding an upside down cross, a black rose and wearing purple hoods; fugitives from justice; paymasters of promises; thieves of corpses or jewels and locks of corpses' hair; terrified kids trying to pass an initiation rite; or some beautiful woman performing the most unthinkable and bizarre acts.

It was a pretty crowded cemetery, no doubt about it. But that's not why it ceased to be like all necropolises at dark, a furtive, silent place, where you talk in a low voice for fear of an echo, of the resonance that summons ghosts. Lavinia and Lisander were not at all afraid of any of those folks (or the ghosts). They just simply didn't want to socialize. They thought everyone should go their own way.

A particular mausoleum might strike them as so beautiful–like that red marble one with wreaths and cherubim, the one belonging to the countess of who knows what–that they'd stay there all night, telling tales about the premature burial they had read about that very afternoon in the first volume of Poe. They'd imagine how many cataleptics would suffer the rigors of asphyxia, the helplessness and the layer of tamped down earth, suffocating emanations, worms lying in wait, and who were at that very moment closed up in their coffins very close by ("Let them rot!" whispered Lisander). They'd finally fall asleep, arms around each other on the cold, polished surface. Little boy and young girl in blue and pink: a tender, Victorian painting by Sir Joshua Reynolds.

That's when the cockroaches would emerge. With absolutely no consideration for human children, so helpless and strangely orphaned, they clambered up in piles as if each one wanted to be the first to get to the booty. Taking a fort while the drawbridge is down. They walked on them, soiled them with their slime and their drool, gnawed their clothes, their nails, their hair... In short, they violated them. Returning home in the morning, Lavinia and Lisander would brush off their pockets and wrinkled clothes. Countless intruders would slip away in every direction, heading for cover. They competed to see who was loaded down with more of them. A big one counted the same as two little ones, a healthy one equaled three broken ones, an albino one was worth four brown ones. They didn't take any antibiotics. They didn't even wash up. You see, Mama and Papa had flown into the eye of the tornado before driving home the point about hate, fear, disgust at the banned household demon, the #1 enemy of housewives and decent people everywhere. Plain and simple, that repulsion wasn't stamped on their superego.

The damp, hot house with half rotten boards, full of nooks and hiding places, suffered from a super population of the undesirable creatures. They swarmed everywhere: floor, roof, walls. They climbed up and down at all hours of the day. Inside the oven, under the washbasin, on top of the soap or the slotted spoon, in the sewing machine drawer, between the sheets. Drowning (or very nearly) in the toilet. In all sizes, shapes and hues. Alone, in pairs or en masse. Where you'd least expect them. After all those years of living with the bugs, Lavinia and Lisander had certainly learned to expect them. Their sharpened senses could detect a motionless winged presence several meters away, in the deepest dark of night.

During their siesta and even during their embrace of discovery, the cockroaches grew bold again, walking on them, contaminating and gnawing. Lavinia's hands would slide down her little brother's spine as he lay on top of her...a cockroach. While he was biting her, gently, there where it hurt the most, he'd look up, to see her face and...a cockroach. The dark, moving smudge, a trail on her transparent white skin. Each one got used to finding something unsettling about how the other tasted. They'd brush off the bugs if they were in the mood; if not, they tolerated them. They could barely make a sudden move, (a quick thrust in the first fluid, a broken hymen) without squashing one. Lisander was convinced that one day when they least expected it they were going to wake up like Gregory Samsa, changed into we already know what...

From the doorstep the man with the machine explained his intentions to the woman. Over and over, like a benefactor, without gesturing and without raising his voice. He showed her his credentials like someone showing off a chimera. Super skinny, emaciated, all skin and bones, kneecaps jutting out and tits, pendulous like a bitch with a lot of litters, wearing a half transparent, filthy robe, she shook her head no. One hand resting on the door frame, the other on her waist, refusal written all over her face.

"No way, sir."

"But it's my job. It's what they pay me for. Maybe you don't realize you've got a problem."

"Nobody here called you, sir."

"Anyone can call. It's a public health concern. Look..."

"There's nothing public in this house, sir. Everything's private. If you want something public, the cemetery is right over there. It's got some beautiful monuments."

"Oh! You don't understand. You want to do things the hard way. Why don't you let me do my job and we'll leave it at that?"

"You're the one who's making things hard, sir. Your only choice is to leave."

"But!"

"I already told you, sir, there are no cockroaches in this house."

"Oh, yeah? What do you call that?"

The man with the machine pointed his triumphant, rigid, accusatory finger at a specimen on the ground, a few steps from the door (on the inside, of course). It seemed to be listening very attentively to the discussion about its fate, like a defendant trying to follow the sophisms and other twisted reasoning bantered about by the defense and the prosecution. The woman looked at it and just laughed nonchanlantly, then looked at the visitor again.

"What about it, sir?"

That attitude of hers, a mixture of apathy, condescension, and insolence, made the man with the machine so indignant that he completely forgot about the aforementioned machine, tanks, tubes, hoses and liquid death and took a step inside, clearly intending to grind the daring bug to a pulp with one stamp of his big foot. But the woman stepped between the man and the bug and shrieked:

"Don't you dare, sir! Don't you dare!" She seemed truly frightened. "You have no right to invade my house!"

"But don't you see that cockroach?"

"Does that mean you've got to squash it? It's the only one. The only one!"

The man with the machine burst out laughing. When all was said and done, that fly in the ointment had a sense of humor.

"The only one? Listen here," he pointed to the demon dot again. "Where there's one, there can be fourteen thousand. They run in packs!"

"Not in this house, sir. That's the only one, I swear. And we love it very much. It's...it's like one of the family..." The man with the machine laughed hard. "You don't believe me? Watch! I'll show you."

Quick as lightning, before the man with the machine (such a busybody, so arrogant, she thought) could stop her, the woman trapped the cockroach with her hand and held it, alive and intact, with just slight pressure, between her index finger and thumb. The little monster opened and closed its jaws, horrified, emitting a very faint cheep, cheep only trained ears could detect, waving its feet, wings, antennae in a tobacco-colored whirlwind.

"See? You've upset it with your threats. Poor thing."

The man with the machine had stopped laughing; his soul and stomach pretty much lurched to a stop, too. He studied the scene, eyes bugged out, his mouth open even wider. Not paying him any attention, the woman *kissed* the cockroach the way you'd kiss a sick baby or a dying lover. She lavished it with caresses also imbued with that indispensable delicacy—resignation, hope—you usually lavish on something ephemeral, something that lasts only the blink of an eye. She cooed, "My little darling" and finally set it down on the floor with the greatest tenderness in the world. The tiny little thing, not at all used to such impassioned display of affection, fled in panic.

The man with the machine fled, too.

Lavinia's shy nature had greatly influenced her obstinate behavior. She knew she was ugly, miserable, and probably infected by a legion of microbes. So very different from the ladies of the hair-raising castles in the Gothic tales that romanticized cold lands, in stories by Von Kleist for example. Ladies white as the moon, sometimes with a wanton blush high on their cheekbones, with slender fingers, wide forehead, aquiline nose and big eyes of a transparent cerulean blue. Some people call that "consumptive beauty." In Lavinia's case it isn't much of a stretch: it was a question of "consumptive ugliness." Bedraggled, dark, emaciated, not at all poetic.

Lavinia didn't feel repugnance for herself or she didn't want to feel it or she endured it with languid dignity that can be seductive, too, on occasion. Certainly she was guessed to be very shrewd when inspiring repugnance in everyone else, vulgar and superstitious people according to her, who lived a ways from the cemetery, and how closely they're connected with the *factum*. At times she had fun with that. Why not? Among her laudable pastimes, none was as pleasant as tormenting the man with the machine. She wouldn't have traded for a million pesos the face of her victim (the man) at the moment of this story's great kiss.

But at other times, her skill got out of control for a few moments until it drove her, like the grimacer or a character from Stevenson, to wonder if it was really a skill or her own nature. This doubt plunged her into a well of melancholy, where one's love for one's self tumbles and tumbles. It drove her to long to be one with the rocks, the broken tombstones, the futile monuments made of marble or bronze out there in the cemetery. To be one with an unfathomable grave and the sadness of not speaking, not eating, not sleeping for several days, constantly looking out the window, her gaze fixed upon the nearest cemetery wall... There, next to the Greek cross carved in relief, where some jokester had painted a swastika. It was too much and she felt furious about not knowing herself, rage over the low, dense clouds that hovered ominously over the house, over Lisander's new indifference, and how he always looked the other way now.

So she took revenge on the vile, disgusting cockroaches that tried to force her out (even though she didn't realize how much). Furious, she jabbed the broomstick into the more populous crannies, gathering spots or hangouts. Armed with a hard rubber sandal, she annihilated them with her blows as they streamed out.

"A little poison here, a little poison there," she muttered to herself, the way she did back in the days when she made up explanations. "What a complete idiot that guy is! This, this is what they need, what those sons of bitches run all over the place looking for! Give a guy a machine and he thinks he's God's chosen! Who cares about that? Not me!! I can kill them, too!! Take that! And that! And that!"

One, two, an entire brood turned to pulp, mushy goo, shells broken like saltines. Agonized waving of antennae and extremities, genocide, massacre, St. Bartholomew's Eve. The ones that managed to escape waited outside for the storm to clear so they could go back in, get back to their routine and put their noses (hairy, waving antennae) to the grindstone, their noble, magic, blessed, inscrutable work of reproducing.

Lisander stayed outside, too, half blind from being inside all the time, a fugitive from the light, bothered by the melee, and his sister's temperament that fluctuated so. That nut case! How well he knew her. After a couple of hours, after sweeping up the remains of the useless slaughter and piling them in mounds on the patio and maybe burning them—the shells took awhile to burn; some people say they can even withstand the atomic bomb—she would curl up in a corner, crying like a blind leper.

He would not console her. No. None of that squeezing and pinching and "Come on, hey, I'm here for you..." He'd want to, of course, but he would stand firm. Like a rock. Like the red marble columns at the mausoleum. Lisander the strong, the indifferent. How quickly things had changed between them... Why couldn't she sleep alone? What about those horrible dreams that ended in howls, where'd they come from? No matter what he did, she wouldn't describe those dreams to him. Why didn't she want to tell him about them? Why did she roll around between the sheets like a mangled cockroach, half alive and half dead? Let *him* console her, that guy she'd brought home! Didn't she talk to him in the back of the cemetery? Didn't they spend most of their time...?

Yes, as I said before, from living so long with roaches, Lisander detected sounds with a hyperesthesia you could classify as morbid. Not even the fluttering of a wing escaped him. As if it were no big thing, he'd glue his ear to the bug-eaten wall that separated him from his sister entangled with "that guy" and he'd seize upon even the lowest, most intricate sound. An aroused sigh, a muffled moan, friction between damp, panting surfaces... At first he suffered, it pained him that Lavinia could do without him. But after a little while, he discovered a much more entertaining way to *do it*. An age-old way that soon became a ritual, one where he didn't just use his hands...

With studied indifference, the boy hummed the old song about the *brujito* who turned into a butterfly thanks to a doctor who went from place to place in a four-engine plane and gave injections without rhyme or reason. What a load of crap! There were more than enough stupid butterflies, but only one *brujito*. Hampered by such gloomy reflections, he would sit down on the stoop, pick a cigarette butt off the ground and light it. Yellowed paper, loose tobacco, gray smoke. He counted the survivors assembled around him like a champion's hunting party, a very easygoing child prince, an *infante* more easily manipulated than the bloodthirsty, cockroach-icidal regent. He told himself, yes, there were more than enough to carry out his ritual, that he and the roaches were out of danger of getting lost in the confused mob of some radical change. Life at the back of the cemetery would continue on its unalterable course.

Lavinia had found only member of her own species to keep company with her, "that guy" she talked to at the grave farthest from the house, "that guy" with whom she... If Lisander was going to abandon her bed to move to the room next door, she'd... The champion no longer wanted any part of all those bones, complaints, distress over bad dreams, kicks in the mouth, getting kneed in his testicles and, to top it off, reticence. He preferred to sleep on the rickety cot or right on the ground. The other thing was, as you'll soon see, he felt he had to deal with all kinds of issues his sister should understand but didn't. Who knows why, but she needed a full time lover. The guy was stooped over, melancholy with a gloomy face, ghoulish, no meat on his bones. No one else would have liked him.

The upstart had a job cleaning floors, bathrooms and bedpans in a cancer hospital, which represented a step up for him; he'd been a gravedigger before. Although the nearly dead made more noise, he preferred them to the dead, all things considered. He was a strange guy who loved life, although he had an extremely broad, very weird concept of it. It never would have occurred to him to change the brujito into a butterfly, or even into a giant moth. He was epileptic with *gran mal* seizures, but his acquaintances took him for feeble-minded. They repeated what they said two or three times, very slowly, very clearly, and he went along with it. They called him "The Mummy" on account of his extraordinary resemblance to the remains Lord Caernarvon and company found so long ago in that sinister chamber where the pharaoh's *ca* roamed, executing meddlers.

Against all odds, he turned out to be a splendid lover. Or at least, adequate. Lovable as the reddish half-dark of mid-afternoon and fogged up mirrors that reflect little or nothing. Mild-mannered, ghostly. Adult. Lavinia's bones didn't bother him one bit (he knew the name of each one and the best way to situate himself among them), nor her mood swings, nor the cockroaches' assaults and retreats, nor her infernal nightmares where Mama and Papa fall down a precipice in a burning car or are tied up, naked, under a spotlight in a torture cell. He embraced her in the brief respite between the atrocity of her dream and the atrocity of her vigil. He whispered in her ear that she shouldn't let such trivia upset her so. Something a lot worse could certainly happen: the Unnamable, he would say and even pronounce the capital letter. What no one can reveal without one's auricles and ventricles bursting.

Nor did he pay much attention to Lisander's clashing jealousy. The boy pretended to ignore him in a thousand curious ways. He didn't say hello. He hid the Phenobarbital so he could get a good look at the Mummy's convulsions, from the beginning of the aura and the small stick wrapped in gauze that Lavinia placed solicitously between his jaws all the way to his blackouts and stupor. He badmouthed people who cleaned floors, bathrooms and bedpans in cancer hospitals with all their howls and rotting flesh and stained rags. He made faces behind his back, mocking his spasms, eyes rolled back, frothing, muscles twitching. He tossed cockroaches in the guy's coffee. Often the Mummy spit out a wing or a sticky paw and even pieces of striped abdomen. Maybe the unstable boy did all this because he missed his sister's little nipples, or rather, the happy times when he slept with them in his hands, squeezing tight after a very soothing walk through the cemetery, dreaming about maple leaves that were still green. The boy had already forgotten the kicks, getting kneed in the groin and the absurd secrecy Lavinia maintained about her oneiric life. Not knowing how to recover what was lost, he zealously dedicated himself to putting his rival's patience to the test.

As I've said, the Mummy didn't get sucked into the game. What's more, he understood. To Lisander's greater humiliation, the Mummy felt proud of himself for understanding.

"He feels displaced, my darling girl, and he's right—up to a point." He justified Lisander's behavior and even defended him when Lavinia took it badly. "He's still so young. He'll get over it."

The incredible Mummy was just that kind of person, perfect for some, nothing surprised him, a guy who goes through life as if he would persevere, and manage not to get singed jumping through the ring of fire of any dirty, perverted (?), inhumane story as if it were the most natural thing in the world, because anything goes, and it's only scandalous if we take it too seriously. He was, in the end, one of those fortunate people who take things as they come, calmly and philosophically.

In a display of that calm spirit, flashing his somewhat sardonic smile (a mummy's smile—did you expect pears from an oak tree?), he showed up one tantrum-filled afternoon, bearing a special gift for Lavinia. "So my darling girl won't cry anymore," he told her as she undid the package and found a mass of tattered organic tissue, a whitish ball, violet in some parts. It looked like it had burst open, with repulsive little blue veins, and covered with protuberances, tiny bumps, pimples; other parts had little hairs. Something resembling intestines or guts seemed to strangle it and it was equipped with an eye (human? or was it a scene right out of that Buñuel movie, *The Andalusian Dog?*) that looked off in the distance. The whole mess was submerged in formaldehyde inside a cylindrical glass container closed tight, about 10 centimeters in height and diameter.

Absorbed in studying such an amazing thing, Lavinia suddenly stopped crying. She turned the flagon a couple of times to find the very best angle so the eye "was looking" right at you. You'd've thought it was going to wink. Excited, the darling girl threw herself on her Mummy (generous, sophisticated, original) to kiss his sunken lips. She clapped, delighted like the young girl she was or like a penguin about to get some fresh fish on an Antarctic morning.

Lisander, as usual, was looking off in the other direction...

After a week of vomiting and confusion and another week of psychiatric care, the man with the machine returned. Perhaps to confirm the degree of verisimilitude (not to say reality) of what happened. Without a doubt, that experience had all the qualities of a delirious, drunken spree with the dregs of the cemetery. The skinny woman was ill and filthy, true, but no matter, what she was, was a person. Human and Earth dweller, Sapiens. And, she was a woman. She *couldn't* have done that.

Or maybe he returned to defend his principles. The skinny girl was free to kiss anyone she wanted, it wasn't right to question her bizarre preference (he was a man with the machine, not a marriage counselor), but he had a job to do. He'd been put on this earth for that and that alone. Obligation, duty, ethics. His sacred professional standards. No one had ever resisted him and that wouldn't start now. No kiss would stop him. They weren't going to slip through his fingers and that was that. Forget about it! What were they thinking? In the end it was he, exorcist, exterminating angel, carrying out a mission in the name of God.

Curious and negative, Lavinia greeted him that day and every day thereafter. Each visit seemed to be the last. But no, he always returned. A journey through our story that keeps on going, never ending like in soap operas. Lavinia came to admire the man's persistence, the growing subtlety of his arguments (he eagerly studied Aristotle's *Rhetoric* and Cicero's *Oratory*), his indomitable faith. She even awaited him, seated in the living room, very composed, like fiancees of yesteryear.

His allegations about cockroaches' malignancies and their overwhelming capacity to reproduce didn't convince her, of course. A geometric progression or something like that: the old saying about the squares on a chessboard or the seeds in the poppy.

"If humans knew how many exist and how many there are to come," the man affirmed throwing around some statistics, "they would fall into the black funnel of a nameless fear. They would never again manage to induce sleep!"

"That doesn't matter, Sir," answered Lavinia. "Even not knowing those facts, it almost always takes a lot of work for me to, as you say, 'induce sleep.' But that part about the black funnel is OK. Keep on talking, if you like. I love listening to you."

Not one to be intimidated, he would return, in his persuasive chatty way, to the first thing that came to mind, fictitious or not, to move him toward his goal. Hence he alluded to that story by Cortázar entitled "House Taken Over," where the owners were forced to retreat. In his version the restless, somnambulant spirits are replaced by cockroaches. He also mentioned an impressive list of illnesses the disgusting critters can transmit.

On that last point the man dug his heels in. Above all when it came to the most visible illnesses, the ones that afflict the skin and connective tissue. The majority of them were barely related to cockroaches, but after all, making connections between very remotely related facts is one of the hallmarks of a good debater. None of them was a doctor--not the skinny girl, not the two guys who leaned over her shoulder, one on each side, to get a peek at the engravings and full color illustrations he showed them: rashes, purulence, herpes, scabs, blisters, boils, necrosis... a dark strip covered each patient's eyes and some of the foreground. The man's charlatanism and his pessimistic, ominous predictions were bolstered by his certainty that doctors, since they know a thing or two, don't normally live in such unhygienic conditions as the ones you could detect, even at a distance, in that home on the verge of being overrun.

Still, nothing worked. Not even by threatening them with that watered down and somewhat dishonest entelechy (Aristotle's term) called the Law, contained in his printed booklet with all its seals and signatures, symbol of authority. The skinny girl examined the booklet for hours with the help of a magnifying glass while the man stood waiting in the doorway, all the weight of the machine on his shoulders, watching cockroaches crossing back and forth with impunity. And there he stood, like a beast of burden, he thought, like a pack mule, powerless to spoil their journey. It would have been so easy! A foamy *phut, phut* and that's that!

But they never invited him to sit down, not even to come in. His place was on the other side, on the threshold. If they offered him coffee, he declined courteously: a cup of coffee is a dark place, suitable for secretly inserting the little body of a very unlucky dead bug. This suspicion made him tremble but he couldn't shake it. Since the day of the kiss, he instinctively distrusted the sordid inhabitants of that house. Could they be trying to draw him into their cult? With their strange attitudes they could have been trying to provoke him as much as convert him. Anyone associated in such a morbid way with insects inevitably sacrifices some pillars of his own humanity along the way, the grandiloquent, modern encyclopedist thought.

The older guy backed up anything the skinny girl decided. She was the most outspoken of that obstinate, necropolitanic family. Her somewhat languid decisions, dictated out of fatigue or even boredom—for example, handing back the booklet and informing him she didn't give a flip if they imposed a fine on her, she'd pay and be done with it—were often were reduced to a single word: no. N-O. No, no, NO. The younger guy, a boy, closed his eyes halfway and didn't say a word.

That's how it went, day after day...

"What's that thing?" Lisander asked, pointing to the jar on the night stand.

It was the quiet and uneasy time of day when the Mummy wasn't around. The boy, rigid with insecurity (the same insecurity that presides over the illegal acts by someone who hasn't yielded to extreme cynicism), took the opportunity to approach his sister. As stiff as if she had swallowed a broom, she egged him on too in that oppressive atmosphere being alone together caused, just the two of them, in the same bedroom, only a few steps apart. They both pretended to be casual, cordial, the old "nothing's going on here." Not even that saved them from the addictive lack of understanding between the heron and crane, of their non-coupling. They didn't like the situation, of course. But each had their own partial and incomplete reasons; susceptible, nevertheless, to joining together like pieces of one lone gear to construct all of Reason. They assumed they had no choice. Can't live with you, can't live without you. A bitter paradox common to characters locked into the same drama, partners in crime. With so much suppressed anxiety, they were like a couple of flies trapped in a spider's web, like puppets worked by a crazy god.

"I don't have a clue," said Lavinia. "But it's cool, isn't it?"

"If you say so..." Lisander forced himself to concede, but for some disconcerting reason, that artifact made him nervous.

"Yes, kiddo, it's cool," she insisted anxiously. "Especially the eye. See? It looks tired. Didn't I tell you Always open! It has no eyelid..."

"Where'd you get it?"

"He gave it to me..." Lavinia sighed. For a few seconds she watched a cockroach settle on Lisander's shoulder like a sailor's parrot and quickly added, "But that doesn't matter. I swear it doesn't. If you want it, I'll give it to you..."

"Where'd he get it?" Lisander deceived himself into believing that a rational explanation would cure his growing anxiety.

"I don't know. From the hospital, I think."

"From the hospital? Then it's HUMAN!!!"

"Where'd you think he got it?" Like in the old days, among the graves, Lavinia couldn't suppress her tendency to be wicked.

"It's human! It's human! It's...!"

"You don't have to say it over and over. You'd think you'd never seen anything human. So, what are you now, an alien?" Lavinia smiled. "I told you, if you want it, you can have it. It's yours."

"I thought... I mean, I... you know..."

Suddenly the boy felt he was being spied on. He jerked around, swallowed and his gaze fell directly on the container, turned to its best angle, Lavinia's favorite. Yes, the eye was looking at him, but it didn't look tired despite the blotches on its sclera. Just the opposite, it looked like it never got tired. Perhaps inquisitive. Or mocking. Piercing. Its iris was brown, its pupil constricted, and it was trained right on him. Ready to trap secrets and uncensored confessions that would slither along the planes and depths of its visual field like earthworms. How could a dead eye have such a fixed look, embedded in that nauseating blob? A stinging, prickly feeling came over his body. A cold metallic, merciless sensation. With one blow Lisander knocked off the cockroach sitting on his shoulder and the bug, dead as a doornail, went tumbling into the coffee cup Lavinia was holding.

"Hey! That's getting old!" she exclaimed, as she fished the bug out by a leg, threw it against the wall and drank her coffee down in one gulp. She wasn't going to let another bug fall in. "Look, kiddo, don't fuck around with me. For the last time, grab that thing and take it with you."

For a few seconds, the boy's mind went blank. How could he explain that that thing scared him, that he wasn't drawn to it, just the opposite? No way did he want it peering at him. His small, evil deeds were his business and no one else's. How could he keep from thinking that the *sum quod eris* could also refer to the mass in formaldehyde, to the sleepless eye turned conscientious objector? Explain that to Lavinia? To the Mummy, who at that moment was sticking his key in the lock? Never! Never ever! Some people are asked questions way beyond their ability to answer, people who destroy their nerves in needless battles with themselves and don't really know why. The moralist—and I'm not one—would say they're paying for something. Crime and punishment. Well then, Lisander was one of these people.

So, to continue the story I have to quote my own words from an earlier page. *With great enthusiasm -and unconfessed terror- her little brother shrugged his shoulders. Only a circumstance that menacing would draw him out of his habitual, excessive reserve. Along with other contemptuous and obscene tough guy grimaces, he would throw caution to the wind and stick out his extremely long tongue -it looked like the tongue of the little devil who tempted St. Simeon Stylites*—stuck out his tongue at the prisoner in the container—before grabbing it and running to his room, pursued by the echo of Lavinia's words:

"Ah, I forgot! Don't toss it out. You can't toss out things that way, you just can't. Don't ask me why...I just know you can't. If you toss it out, it comes back. Be better to give it to someone else..."

Caught up in his own deed and in keeping his heart from leaping out of his chest, Lisander, number one tough guy, didn't hear the brief dialogue that followed between his sister and the Mummy who'd just arrived. "Are you upset?"

"No, of course not. When in all the time you've known me have you seen me upset?"

"Oh! One of these days I'm going to get bored with both of you. You because you understand everything and him because he doesn't understand a thing..."

"I don't understand everything, my darling girl. Don't believe that for a second. For example, I don't understand why you said that bit about if he tossed it out, it'd come back. What's that about?"

"That's foolishness, silly. Pure imagination. Lisander is destructive, I know him, he uses up things he likes and I'd like him to at least hang on to your gift. The bottom line is he has no one to give it to. He doesn't know a soul. Just you and me. OK?"

"OK, no problem. You know something, my darling girl? I love it when you say 'I would like...' Isn't there something else you'd like?"

At that point Lisander plugged up his ears. He'd set the Cyclops in a corner, then wished to God he hadn't! Lavinia laughed like a

master of derision and, between sighs, told the Mummy everything she wanted at that moment (almost the same thing Lisander
had been wanting in vain for so many months), naming body parts
and actions related to those body parts in the lewdest and most
exciting way she could think of.

Just like any other loner would in his place and in full posses-
sion of his mental faculties, as the saying goes, the boy would have
listened quietly a while longer till he got an erection (big waves of
pleasure stirred him to his feet) and a damp foreskin. He would
have looked for an old brown paper sack under the mattress, captured four or five cockroaches, then sealed them up inside despite
their struggles and their cheep cheeping in protest. His ear always
alert to the events on the other side of the worm-eaten wall, he
would have undone buttons with one hand to liberate what was
already struggling to be liberated and would have stuck it into the
sack. He would barely touch himself, since the fascinating thing
was feeling, all the way to the tip, the scrambling of the bugs as
they walked on it, soiled it, gnawed on it. A slow, minute pleasure,
four or five bugs zigzagging around at the same time, desperate for
the last dregs of air. His ritual.

That's the way it would have been (that's what he'd planned)
except for the presence of the fiendish Cyclops watching him from
its corner. Yes, it was watching him, condemning him without a
trace of the ultimate bonhomie we can find in our *doppelgänger*.
Another kind of erection took hold of him, something like a bod-
iless finger that pointed to its victim with all the insistence, the
evil, the fury of Akinari or Sheridan Le Fanu's vengeful ghosts.
Stories to read in the daylight. Again the stinging, the nibble, nibble all over his body. The cold, metallic, pitiless feeling. Lisander
felt like he was drowning, everything around him was turning
black in a sudden, unrestrained amanuenses, a spark of memory
that appears in a whirlwind of distorted features, cries begging for
help, dangling silhouettes...of Mama and Papa.

His night went on forever.

"Don't be like that. Let me see."

The man with the machine held the container very carefully. It was the second most repulsive thing he had seen in his life, at least up close. In recent times he had learned that supreme disgust, the kind that makes you retch, shake, gives you chills, makes your hair stand on end and for a few moments blends with fear, doesn't originate from objects themselves, but from what human beings do with them. What function and even form bestow upon them. In this last case, supreme disgust is directed at certain aspects of human beings. Those who turn up their nose resist discovering their true reflection.

For example, who came up with the idea of preserving *that* in formaldehyde, rescuing it from its natural disintegration? Who would have held it right in his hands? A biologist, a taxidermist, a lunatic? Any of the above. In any case it was the work of someone like that. With a mixture of anxiety and right now gratitude, the elderly boy was looking at them--at the thing with the eye and at its new caretaker, florescence, sparks flying back and forth.

True, the contents of the container were murky. Vaguely resembling some suspenseful short film the man with the machine had seen months before on his favorite TV show, on Wednesday nights, sitting on his comfortable sofa in his comfortable living room in his comfortable and thoroughly de-cockroached apartment. Something by Orson Welles? That guy had an imagination! Or Hitchcock? Or some imitator? He didn't remember and he didn't care to.

The contents of the container—he didn't dare call it anything else, even at the risk of committing the sin of warped, reflective monotony and poverty of language—was what you'd call despicable. What kind of people are these folks living at the back of the cemetery! But also it was a ray of light on the path of his frustrated machine, the hope he might one day enter that "little shop of horrors" to spread poison right and left. In short, he could certainly take it away, toss it in the first trash can and be done with it. If that would calm down the trembling, deranged guy standing before him... If he interceded on his behalf with the skinny girl...

He couldn't say to the elderly boy (since he didn't know) that the dead matter in the jar was as dangerous as a lyrical abstraction of the blue horseman or a surrealistic jumble from the next decade, that the eye was staring agonized into the eyes of the anonymous artist, but it didn't see his secrets and was even less capable of talking or punishing. The Mummy had actually taken it with love in his heart because, in some terrifying way, it looked pretty and fascinating. In effect it was a wedding present, something Lavinia treasured. She, in turn, had given it to him, to Lisander, to tell him in her macabre, excessively subtle way, just like with the letters, the postcards, the dried-up sheets of paper from childhood, the caresses, the heartbreak and the pleasure of receiving something so forbidden, that she still loved him more than anyone else. To tell him he was the most important thing in the world to her.

Translated by Pamela Carmell.

Fifita Calls Us in the Morning

Mirta Yáñez

I have no idea who Fifita was, but absolutely everybody was singing that song the day we left Havana. And we kept on singing it along the way in the bus, and when we changed the bus for a truck in Cueto and had to put cardboard and bags over our heads because no one had thought to put their rain gear at the top of their packs where it would be easy to get to, but rather at the very bottom. We still felt like singing the same happy little tune, even though nobody else knew who Fifita was either.

What we did know was that Fifita had to be a wild one. Because according to the lyrics of the song, she would wake everybody up at five o'clock in the morning to go and pick coffee. And that is hilarious. With how cold it was in the hills of Mayarí Arriba, not even Fifita could have gotten up anyone from our brigade before six a.m. And getting up at six was hard enough. To top it all off, there was always someone who would start to sing and would have that ditty on their lips from the moment they stepped out of the hammock.

But the story I'm going to tell is about the time that we all got up at five in the morning without a soul, not even Fifita from the song, having to wake us up. It was the morning that the cyclone came and blew down our house.

The previous afternoon had been strange, and when I say strange don't think that I believe in premonitions or anything of the sort; but it's true that even the animals were acting weird, not wanting to come close to anyone Even the house pets, the dogs that normally were so affectionate with me, didn't want to be scratched or even petted on the head. And the fact is that every one of us had a bad feeling about it. I don't know if it was the sky turning red, or the air hanging so heavily, or what. But not even a leaf was moving. And not one of us, of the girls from the brigade I mean, felt like doing a darn thing. And usually every afternoon we'd start wanting to build a bonfire and sing, or play dominoes with the boys, the ones from the boys' brigade who lived just down the road and would come to visit in the afternoons, after they cleaned up.

That's why I said that afternoon something strange was going on, because none of us wanted to sing, not even Maria Luisa, who nobody can get to shut up. And I didn't really feel like petting the dogs anyway, even though I didn't like it that now they didn't want anything to do with me, when they always wanted attention and would follow me barking through the coffee fields, and now when I would try to get near them they would run away and hide under the bushes. No one wanted to stir from their hammocks on account of that weight that hung in the air, like I said.

Well, that afternoon it happened that the sky turned red from one side to the other, not just where the sun goes down, and not even the boys who were living just around the corner came over. But the strangest thing, I mean really, was that we were happy that they hadn't come, so we didn't have to move a muscle, go figure.

So we all went to sleep early, because what were we going to do of we were awake, since the afternoon had begun to get nasty. And that heaviness that came from who knows where, had stirred up a very disturbing breeze. Ibrahim, the house's owner, had said that it meant a storm was coming, and that we should bring in the clothes from the line. Although I tell you, that day nobody had even washed anything, because it was such a bizarre afternoon.

And I remember that I kept on waking up every so often because of the noises the wind was making outside, or because of the cold draft that would work its way into my hammock, in spite of the fact that I had lined it with plantain leaves, since doing it with newspaper like my papa had said didn't work at all, being that I move around a lot when I sleep and the shifting papers make some kind of racket, besides which after three days not a piece of paper was left in place. So I thought up the notion of the plantain leaves that don't make any noise to speak of, and they helped some, but not even that kept me warm that night; and one of the times I woke up I realized that it had started to rain hard and I thought with that deluge we weren't going to be able to go into the fields the next day. Don't tell anybody, but it sounded so good, the idea of sleeping the morning away, with nothing to worry about, wrapped up in my dry bedspread, without changing clothes or pulling on my boots, even if later it would be worse to have to wade into the wet and muddy coffee plantation. That's when I heard a crash and I saw that the side wall had caved in completely and we were at the mercy of the storm.

It seems that night nobody had been able to sleep well, because in the blink of an eye the entire brigade had jumped out of the hammocks and was upright, getting ready for who knows what. And it was when I had started to stuff my clothes into my pack so that they didn't get all wet on me that somebody spoke, because nobody had said a word until then, and it seemed to be like a question that didn't have anything to do with anything, because who cared in that moment if what was streaming in through the hole in the wall looked like a wave that you see in one of those movies of a ship sinking. And who cared what Silina was asking, about where had the tree gone that used to be in front of the house? I thought, what in the world is the matter with her, as if a tree, a júcaro of that size could go anywhere. And I went over to where she was standing and looking, her mouth hanging open, and I thought that for a fact I was going crazy too, because the enormous tree, that must have been about a thousand years old, for all I know, was no longer in front of the house. And after a few minutes, as a bolt of lightning lit up the scene, we saw it knocked over, with its roots in the air, roots so big that they scared you. Now don't you go tell a soul, but I had such a shiver go up and down my spine, I don't know what Silina must have been thinking after that lightning bolt, but what was rolling around in my head was that if instead of falling into the road that tree had fallen toward the house, well, it would have buried us in our beds, hammocks and all, and goodnight Irene. And if Silina was thinking the same thing, she didn't say a word either, so as not to frighten the others who hadn't heard her question and had no idea that the tree was no longer where we had left it in the afternoon.

That's when Ibrahim showed up and told us that we had to get out of there. I stuffed a bedspread and a padded shirt into my knapsack, wrapped up in the only waterproof jacket that I had, and it didn't even occur to me to pack anything else. So I put on the same clothes that I wore every day in the fields and when I turned around I saw that the entire brigade was ready to leave the house, and once again that night I recalled the shipwrecks in the movies, when the captain would go below deck and say that the storm was blowing up, to tie down the sails and everyone take cover. Women and children to the lifeboats first. And in thinking of that, I walked out into the driving rain.

I had never seen anything like it. When I tell you that the palm trees were bending over as if they were cardboard, none of you will believe me. The wind was knocking them down, it looked like they would split in half, and then they would pop back up like nothing had happened, then double over again, and from time to time a tree limb would come free and fly off as if it had a life of its own. I swear that in that moment I saw the loose stalks sweeping by and I didn't hardly think about the branches, or the palm fronds that were swaying like lengths of thread, or about the rain beating down everywhere, because of the five dogs that were milling around my feet and wouldn't let me take a step, the same dogs that wouldn't let me near them that afternoon, you know how animals are. And sometimes the branches would sail over and land right next to us in the road, because what I haven't mentioned yet is that the boys had been waiting outside to walk with us to the town, and that the town was about four miles away over the mountain paths.

And I'm sure that when we took the turnoff we were all together; I don't know what happened up the trail, but we ended up spaced farther apart, and all of a sudden you couldn't see three feet in front of you, what with the dark and how hard the rain was coming down, and only when a streak of lightning would cross the sky could you see a thing. And what you saw was the palm trees bending over the road, and the fluttering sounds in the air sounded like birds, but you knew they were tree limbs. But that didn't bother me, nor did the fact that I was in the middle of the mountain, all alone, trudging up and down hills in the midst of a downpour, because everybody else had gone on ahead, and I had fallen way behind on account of the dogs. The truth is that as I'm telling it right now, I don't even believe myself. It's probably just that I wasn't aware that the storm was Hurricane Flora, and I hadn't read anything about what they were saying in the papers those days, so I didn't really understand what was going on.

The only thing I thought about was that our wall had fallen down, that I had forgotten Manolo's letters, and that now they were probably getting drenched back there at Ibrahim's house, and about the dogs that were beside me, getting tangled up in my feet so that I couldn't walk. Although it wasn't completely their fault, because sometimes walking against the wind I couldn't move forward at all, and I couldn't open my eyes all the way on account of the rain would get in them and sting. I asked myself, from time to time, where the rest of them had gotten to, since I couldn't hear them any more. And then I'd start to think again about what I was going to tell Manolo when he mentioned the letters and I'd have to tell him that I hadn't remembered them at all when I saw the tree upside down and the wall that had fallen in, and we had to be evacuated to the town that was four miles walking through the mountains. And sure enough he wouldn't believe that now I was thinking about the letters that were getting wetter in the house as I was walking through the downpour.

And then, if that wasn't enough, some pebbles had gotten into my boots, and what with the strange things that go through your mind in those circumstances, and the stranger things that you do, when I saw that I wasn't going to be able to get up the last hill before the town because of the force of the water streaming down it, and the stones were bothering my feet, I sat down at the edge of the path and untied the laces of my boots and even took off my socks to pour out the rocks and the mud that had seeped in. And then I started petting the dogs, who were really nervous and antsy. I started imagining that maybe the water wouldn't rise up in the house too much and my backpack would be saved from the flood, so that Manolo wouldn't get mad at me because his letters had been lost in the shipwreck. And I envisioned Manolo dressed up as a sailor shouting *women and dogs to the lifeboats,* which made me want to laugh, and there I was laughing when Raphael appeared and grabbed me by the elbow and helped me get up the hill.

When we came to the top, to the town, the rest were waiting for us. What did you think, I asked, that I had drowned in the flood? But nobody laughed, instead they stared at me, scared. And that's how I found out that they had arrived like an hour before, and I didn't show up, and they thought that maybe a limb had fallen on me, like that guy over there, wounded, because a palm trunk had broken three of his ribs, who they happened to find by accident in the dark. And I told them that it was that some little stones in my boots were bothering me and had Manolo's letters gotten all wet, and the dogs... But truth be told my knees were starting to buckle under me from fright, even though I don't think anyone noticed, because what can I say, you have to keep it together till the end, so I burst into laughter and asked if that so-called Fifita had gotten up yet, because between you and me, that little Fifita song was starting to be a drag.

Translated by Sara E. Cooper.

Past Meets Present: Odd Tales Out of School

Mirta Yáñez

Telling a Christmas Tale

For Camila Henríquez Ureña, in memorium

He wakes up and at first doesn't know where he is. From the second floor of the building you can hear a noise like...little pebbles falling one by one. A mottled light floods the corridor to the right.

The character, a professor, is alone in the Department in the wee hours of the 25th of December. He is always the last one to leave and tonight has fallen asleep after checking the halls and turning off lights in classrooms and offices. It occurs to him that the only light that should still be on is in the lobby. So, suddenly surprised, he shakes off the vestiges of sleep. He inspects the breaker box and checks that all the circuit switches are set to off.

He thinks of picking up the phone. It's three o'clock in the morning and the city sleeps. But even if it were twelve noon he wouldn't know who to call. Looking outside, the night seems grim. The entranceway and the intersection of Zapata and Avenue G, with the huge trees in shadow, are briefly illuminated with the changing traffic light. In comparison, the old building that houses the Humanities feels shockingly warm and friendly.

From the hallway to the right, in the direction of the Department of Hispanic Literatures (his own), spills a nebulous gleam, and that sound of the smallest pebbles dropping.

It is Christmas Eve, he remembers, the night that according to legend shades and specters show themselves. The character is not that interested in the border that links the world of the dead with the world of the living. A presence from the beyond is the last thing he would think about. He himself, during the last ten years, has turned into a soul in penance. The living dead, which is the worst.

The professor has just turned fifty, is all alone, the city is falling to pieces all around him, he no longer likes his classes, and the daily routine is rending him like a meat grinder. Desperation and boredom parch his free moments, the few that are left to him in the exhaustion of survival in turn-of-the-century Havana.

He decides to investigate what's happening up on the other floor. He climbs the stairs, crosses the threshold of the conference room, and walks toward the Department office. When he opens the door, it seems that he sees what he always does: built in book- shelves along the wall, a rolling table with a decrepit typewriter, a desk, a few seats, and the piece that they call "Camila's armchair." The only thing different is that dusty light coming out of nowhere and that noise, that he still can't quite place, intermittent, less audible now because of his own shuffling steps.

Something strange is going on there. By nature the character doesn't believe in any of that hocus pocus or mumbo jumbo. However, because of his profession he has read, studied, even meditated on those beings that sometimes seem to return, having left loose ends, to answer a call, to exact a punishment. Whatever the case, the professor perceives that the presence is benevolent.

He stops in front of the armchair. That rustling, that rhythm. That soft sound, now he recognizes it. It's the whispering of the turning, one after another, of the pages of a book. Fltt, one sheet, a pause, fltt, another page turned, another interval, fltt, the next page... It's reading!

The chimera, the ghost, whatever it is, is reading.

The professor slips out of the department office and softly closes the door. He doesn't want to interrupt. He understands that just like the living, or perhaps more, the presence was longing for her books. He realizes that she has come to say her final goodbye, one last act: she hadn't managed to finish what she was reading.

The character returns to his place in the lobby. Wrapped up in his own thoughts, he listens to the rustling of pages turning and finds serenity, he doesn't feel alone, or rather he feels comforted in his solitude for the first time in a long time. He pieces back together an old inner harmony; that soft sound replenishes him with a peace that he had almost forgotten. He is overcome with the urge to reread those beloved books that he has left dusty in his bookcase for so long. Dawn breaks on Christmas day. They say that sometimes our dead guide us along the path of life.

Nothing Save the Airs

Everything was falling into place. I had time to kill, and the Morgan Library on the corner of Madison and 36th was only eight blocks from Bryant Park, where I had a date with K. I hadn't been able to pass up the opportunity that chance had provided to see with my own eyes Poe's manuscripts, the spidery and nervous calligraphy that had penned the word *nevermore*.

Still shaken up by my recent proximity to the maestro, I walked down 5th Avenue to 42nd Street. No one seemed to notice that a raven was flying along right behind me.

And there I was, darkly contemplating the theme of abandonment, on a bench in Bryant Park, as that chilly spring New York afternoon drew to a close. K. still hadn't arrived, and I think that she never did. Although it was all the same to me; overhead, in the trees' bare branches, keeping me company, was the Raven.

"Raven forlorn, raven all alone," said the vagrant. He wasn't talking to anyone in particular. He was dressed all in black; as, as a matter of fact, was I (and the majority of New York's inhabitants). From a plastic bottle he slowly sipped a clear liquid that looked like water, but smelled like cheap rotgut. He chain smoked cigarettes that he would take out of a little case propped on top of a bundle of papers and rags nestled in a grocery store cart, where apparently he carried all his worldly possessions.

The air grew strangely still, and the Raven let out a piercing squawk. The vagabond pointed a finger at me and asked:

"Have you ever cursed the gods?"

I answered sincerely that I hadn't, with a shake of the head.

"Have you drunk until you were plunged into the depths of unconsciousness?"

Again, I denied it.

The vagrant frowned disapprovingly, and it occurred to me that I wasn't going to pass the test. He gave me one more chance:

"Have you ever tried to drown your emotional anguish with physical pain?"

Relieved, I responded that I had.

The transient gave the Raven a look of complicity. "Certainties," he said, "always engender suffering, whatever the truth that may have been revealed. Van Gogh..." and with a hand so pale that the veins showed through, he made a gesture suggesting the flight of a flock of birds in the gloaming, "the last year of his life he painted ravens in a field of wheat. Ravens don't leave you."

Without my noticing, night had fallen. I wanted to return to the natural order of things, to the people strolling or rushing by. Then the vagabond, as if to indicate that the conversation was over, quoted from memory the same lines I had just read, a few hours ago, in the Morgan Library: "Nothing save the airs that brood over the magic solitude." He looked at me, and I paled, as if I had seen a ghost.

Anagnorisis

The bell had barely rung when the aging professor—or the *Doctora*, as she was usually called for her devotion beyond the call of duty—walked into the classroom on the fourth floor of the college, precisely the room right next to the elevator, with improvised partitions and blackboards that had seen better days, a room whose august scenery was being worn down by the demands of the passing years.

The *Doctora* commenced her lecture on "The Decadence of Literature in the Twentieth Century" in the same morose tone of voice that had made her famous with generation after generation of students.

Suddenly, maybe on account of the exasperating heat in the room, or perhaps due to waves of an inclement menopause, the *Doctora* excused herself from the podium only to return a half an hour later with her hair streaming water, her clothing soaked through, and exuding an inexplicable scent of wet grass, as if she had been dancing through the pastures in a downpour.

The students, terrified, applied themselves furiously to their studies and earned higher grades than had ever been documented in the history of the course. The university administration decided to officially commend the *Doctora*, and during the very act of homage the venerable walls of the Aula Magna fell down amidst the thankful moos of the last of the Sacred Cows.

Translated by Sara E. Cooper.

Mare Atlanticum

Mylene Fernández Pintado

"Silvio and Aute are at the Plaza de las Ventas. Wouldn't you like to go?"

"I'm tired of Silvio. I think I listened to him too much when I was a teenager."

But you begin to praise him, and you're quite right. I sit on the couch in a skeptical pose while inside me grows something that might be common and childish pride. Silvio is mine. That's why I can concede myself the luxury of a bored shrug while you hang on every chord and every word.

He's mine in this city where I've got nobody to call on the phone, no friend to introduce you to who'll introduce you to some small part of me. This city without my hideaways, my old photos, or scribbles that give away my flights of teenage fancy. This city where all I've got is short stretches of you. This Madrid, that took me just a week to get used to but will always be alien, as alien to me as the Havana of rum, salsa, and plantains.

"You really don't want to go?"

Don't try to convince me. We made a devil's pact that day, believing in the foolish notion that love conquers all. Each will respect the private life of the other, we said, and now we can't concede ourselves the luxury of making demands. You have your friends, students, family, and former girlfriends. All your past, much of the present, and the uncertainty of the future. I have my memories, including the ones I share with you, my silences, and my doubts. I have that Havana which my longing has stripped of its daily disadvantages, and I have the certainty of being a foreigner here. We talk, and the December light disappears from the living room while our conversation becomes more intimate, as if the sun did not wish to witness the last and most painful confessions we make. There are no reproaches. We tally up all the good things we've invested in this effort we refuse to consider unsuccessful, though it has nothing to do with the small doses of happiness we promised ourselves when we had faith that six time zones and some minor variations in obscenities were not windmills we should find particularly threatening.

The radical differences one accepts, enjoys, and does not try to eliminate, but each small discrepancy becomes a bottomless abyss. Like stigmata against the background of so many ways we're compatible, they cover over our daily language with cryptic hieroglyphics we do not understand.

"Could I use a knife and fork instead of chopsticks?" I asked hopefully on the eve of the dinner you organized to celebrate the solstice and the arrival of winter.

I sat at the table and invoked neither Buddha nor Basho nor Mishima nor Kurosawa, but rather those other gods in whom I had always refused to believe for fear of seeming uncivilized. I didn't care what the rest of the diners thought. They would surely be more generous than you, or maybe they were suffering my same difficulties only for them these constituted a delicious Western awkwardness whereas in me they testified to a terrible isolation from the world.

"No, never. It's the first time I've eaten with chopsticks. First time I've eaten Japanese food, too." And I looked at you, saw I had passed and with high marks too. I felt so happy I flirted all night with your friends. Exotic me, speaking in my unusual rhythm and coming from that place about which they all knew enough to be hungry for more. All of this so as to be *maja* and *guapa*, a fun-loving girl who could please you by pleasing your friends. So I thought, exhausted, while clearing away mountains of exquisite porcelain, the last Labor of Hercules before we could once more be ourselves—until the next telephone call or the next class to teach.

We feel guilty. I, for having made you believe as I did that you were more important than the person at your side who I no longer am. You, for having torn me from that place toward which you profess such mixed feelings. I'm tired of reciting a part in dialogues which are not mine, you of translating names, facts, and allusions. I'm tired of feeling tribal, perpetually and primitively surprised. You're fed up with taking care of me so that so much strangeness doesn't do me in.

That dinner for your family: they showed up when we were still in our aprons, having spent the afternoon together in preparation, listening to *Al final de este viaje* and skinning great piles of fava beans while you filled me in on the invitees with sharp observations and diagnoses a la Woody Allen. But their only comment on the food was how good beans could taste with their skins intact. "Haven't you two ever tried them that way?"

They gave me the world's friendliest interrogation, and I was the charming suspect who confessed to living in a foreign land. But not the way you think. If you could sink your hands into the hot and humid air of my city you would feel what I'm saying, not feel obliged to understand it. Your benevolence toward the faults of my place shows the limits imposed by your distance. I sport no halo, am no immaculate Virgin, wear no revolutionary cap. I can't repeat the language of pamphlets, although you may think that amounts to a betrayal of what's mine, what's ours, what's yours.

When we get angry we get melodramatic too. We hide behind our differences, use them as doors to which one alone has the key. My tourist-hustling *jineteras* become warrior princesses to whose perfect, sensual ambushes of lust and *joie de vivre* your fat, provincial taxi drivers succumb. But the taxi drivers are pyrrhic booty, for the *jineteras* go on to fall into the rude trap repeated *ad infinitum*

since the times of the Conquest. It has always been a time of conquest. They're dazzled by suitcases full of junk from bargain stores.
When all's said and done, Spain is First World and Old World and
now a communitarian state that issues the iridescent "Schengen
Visa," passport to most of Europe.

My plane from Cuba: crammed with subjects intoxicated by the
tropics, full of Cuban rum and creole hips. They tried to hold
onto Havana, prolong the party as long as possible, while I tried
to forget they occupied the same space as you. I tried to grow up,
as if six hours could be six centuries. Lovers are not from any
place, I thought, only from the kingdom of things they have
shared and lived. I found our lucky star in some part of the sky
and entrusted to it our future of mirrors and glass.

Then came the immigration official, a xenophobe who didn't
want any more Cubans fleeing the American embargo by way of
married exile in Spain. "Yes. I'm married," I told him—wanting to
cry and to leave because Madrid did not deserve me. But there you
were, waiting, and when you burst out laughing at my fragile figure
wrapped in an enormous coat, I knew I could circle the world and
all its hours, provided we took each other by the hand and by
storm.

When we're lovers, we're on a swing, and you've discovered infinite positions for making love during our ingeniously idle and
enjoyable afternoons. The swing hangs from the sky, rocking back
and forth between the Prado of your city and the Prado of mine,
where each of us tries to stop it. But it's not anywhere for long,
except the sea in between: the sea which joins and separates,
which communicates and swallows according to our mood, dispo-
sition, or state of love. When we're in love I'm a Caribbean
Scheherezade who spins crazy nonsense stories that are the purest
truth, while you narrate your Marco Polo travels across the island
that fascinates you. We discover that we're not so much from anywhere as from our own tentative little fief.

We've tried to construct an island midway in the Atlantic,
which would have something of Neruda's and Kundera's Prague,
Kiarostami's cherries, the mornings of Cat Stevens and the horror

of onions we share. An island built of the things that take us away from where we're from and bring us closer to one another, an island we've built but can't inhabit. We've distanced ourselves from the differences that made us complementary. We haven't achieved the harmony that makes us alike.

On our first Christmas Eve we went out for a walk. I wanted to see this city on *Nochebuena*, as I didn't remember having seen mine. We came home convinced we were the only spectators in a Madrid with streets decked out for visitors who never arrive. Sidewalks deserted, stores closed; this night was for family, not curious passersby.

You made dinner, your meticulous perfectionist hands filling the kitchen with unknown smells and names. We ate something you invented for me. The candlelight semi-darkness almost worked the miracle of hiding our differences. Almost. We were exquisite and refined diners from some elegant, harmonic set.

One never finishes growing up. Some resistence to adulthood always remains, embedded in a gesture, a last rebellion against the passage of time which, for being so unidirectional and irreversible, thinks itself so clever too.

I open the presents as eagerly as a child enchanted by Melchor, my favorite of the Magi. You watch my hands and face, to steal this moment that stars my childish, awkward self. At the stroke of midnight, Peter Pan opens a treacherous gift from Captain Hook.

Your presents will make me a grandmother with drawers full of treasures to delight my grandchildren. Treasures made in Prague, in Sapporo, or Istanbul so as to someday pass from your hands to mine as silent, gossipy messengers—reminders that some things just don't fit together. Still?

A wooden box. On the cover, a map from 1492: Spain, America, and the routes that cross the *Mare Atlanticum*. It's not so far, you say, while I'm drowning in every drop of water splashed by the prow of that painted caravel, water which floods inside me as if I were drinking it in slow agony.

Five hundred years later, you disembarked from an Iberia jet-liner with a tourist map in hand, and Havana was once again the most beautiful land that human eyes had ever seen. It's not so far. Nine hours flying against the hands of the clock—against the uni-directionality and irreversibility of time.

I open the box's tiny, delicate clasp. Inside there's a sundial with a compass in the middle. I look, one at a time, at the map, the sun-dial, and magnetic north. Circumstantial complements of time and space. Where are we? Will this compass do us any good? Which of us will be the needle for the other? At what point on this map will we halt our anxious ships? At what moment will you, Mad Hatter, or I, White Rabbit, stop time?

I cried all the waves of the Atlantic, all the summer downpours of my country and all the winter drizzle of yours.

"I want to hear this song." Silvio was singing for everyone's Christmas, and I loved you for your stubborn addiction to my music, my poetry; for giving me the chance to cradle you in my Havana lap with the inveterate indulgence that tolerant mothers show capricious sons. That was my Christmas present to you.

It's night now, and our schedules take over our lives. You're going to the concert, and I'm finishing a book by Joseph Roth. The concert will be full of Cubans, you tell me. It will be like going to the Film Festival. But I think it will be Madrid's version of Miami's nostalgia. If I wanted to stick with *cubaneo* I would have stayed in Havana where it's brewed.

You close the door and I hear your steps descend the wooden staircase. You're going without me. How many places won't I be able to accompany you even if I do go along? I look at the city through the windows. The small balconies' crochet-work grills still remind me of that TV series about Fortunata and Jacinta. Madrid is temperate even in winter. If there were a sea here, it would be quiet and gray.

I curl up on the couch because all the cold of the Gran Vía is in my head. And I think of Silvio, the lights, the worshipful crowd that sings along to the tunes I've known since my adolescence, songs heard while sitting on the floor of someone's house, on the wall of the Malecón, tunes coaxed clumsily from the guitars of friends, loved ones, or strangers. Silvio won't know about me. He won't know that here, among this crowd following him as Theseus followed the thread through the labyrinth, this audience hypnotized by a feminine, moist, and demanding Havana, am I, who am Old Havana and Fifth Avenue. He won't know that we repent the same mortal sins we didn't commit, and that his love song *Ojalá* is the most powerful curse in the world.

I'm not one of those for whom he's the marvelous poet of beautiful and strongly felt songs in the world's most exquisite language. I'm one of those who've hated him for being clumsy or vulgar yet have pardoned his small vanities. Theirs is the virtuoso, ours full of the defects that only what belongs to us completely and in our hearts can have. Havana is more than radiant sun and friendly people happy all the time. It's also gray, sad, and complicated. Not the technicolor hues of the postcards, but the colors of Chagall's oils, and of the dying painter in Silvio's song.

I look at my watch and see that the concert has begun. The one by the Silvio I've given you as a present, as I like to give you all the good of my place, of my time in that city where the unforeseen is the best synonym for plans and where chance is always better organized than anything else.

Now I turn out all the lights and feel my way to the stereo where you spent the afternoon listening to *Mujeres* while I tried to understand what the Golden Section in Renaissance painting meant. I push "play" and raise the volume so no one can hear what he and I have to say. What he says to me isn't what he's saying in the Plaza de Toros de las Ventas. Our shared spaces and confederate moments. To evoke them before foreigners would be a sacrilege.

That's why we have to commune without witnesses. So you can go on being the same as when you were the soundtrack of my life in my city, not a fragile and shaky bridge pointing in that direction. You're what's in that metal box, and I'm a loud and laughing teenage girl, not a woman who only whispers and smiles.

Translated by Dick Cluster.

The Anteater

Mylene Fernández Pintado

"If it looks like it's going to be tough, then include your sister in our outing. But only if it's getting tough, okay?"

I obediently agreed to this and the rest of the torrent of instructions issued by the fifteen-year-old strategist who had foreseen solutions for every imaginable eventuality, like a human flow chart. The hardest task, though, belonged to me as executor of the plans. The idea of asking my parents for permission to go out alone with K was terrifying. I think my guilty face alone would have invited a denial.

I was a very sheltered adolescent. In return for a series of material comforts (perhaps envied by my acquaintances), I had to forswear any dream of being a female James Dean. I carefully avoided provoking generational conflicts, such as refusing to accompany my parents on their outings or complaining about their strictness. When they would forbid something, I'd choose to regard that activity as being of little importance. So I modified this request slightly, in the hopes of obtaining more encouraging results for the "crusade."

"Mama, do you think Lili and I can go with K to the zoo on Tuesday?"

My mother was a young and beautiful woman-child who needed to impose absurd fiats in order to reinforce her inexplicably low self-esteem. She was hard to please, but very important within the family, so we all babied her a bit.

"Since when are you interested in animals? Your biology grades are always your worst."

As a student, I really left nothing to be desired, yet my vacations were those of a juvenile delinquent out on personal recognizance: always accompanied, always watched. My going-steady with K, now over a year in length, was limited to listening to music and dubbing tapes while seated in the living room by day or out on the balcony by night. That restricted regime produced two very different effects. In K's eyes, it had made me someone very desirable, a Venus in jeans atop a five-story pedestal. To me, it made him an attentive prince—romantic, safe, and full of story-book love (Cinderella, to judge from the incident of seeking permission to go out). So our relationship advanced in two directions under my parents' attentive and inexorable gaze.

"K says they just got an anteater. I think it's the first new animal in like a century. We want to see it."

"I don't know, ask your father. I'm not too convinced."

My father was always traveling, never home. When he arrived, he was a breath of fresh air and good cheer, full of jokes and presents. He left my mother in charge of maintaining iron discipline, while his role was to be the obliging, understanding one. He rarely intervened, but this time he did.

"Okay. Take your sister, and don't get home late."

I couldn't believe we'd be going out alone. I spent the rest of the day helping around the house. I washed the dishes, didn't talk back to my mother or fight with my sister. I laid out my clothes and went to bed early.

We never found the anteater, despite a thousand twists and turns. I wanted everyone from school to see me, alone with K like the rest of the couples I knew. My sister lagged behind with a stick of cotton candy, happy as a clam. "Let's go to my house, rest a while, then take you home. So you can see it. You've never visited our new house."

The house was pretty, white and full of plants, and K turned out to be a gracious host. "Look, Lili, a tape of ABBA. If you want to hear it, the cassette player's over there. Come on, let's go see the newborn kittens. They're in the garage. They were just born yesterday. I helped the mother give birth."

When we went down to the garage and saw the kittens, I realized we'd come to do "that." What all the teenage girls talked about with longing and fear. The fixture of conversation among my friends at school, the great unknown of our lives. Where would it be? With whom? How? Indeed, we had our preconceived ideas about this event. We were full of plans and suggestions and, above all, we were sure that it would occur before marriage. Myself, I imagined that the ceremony had certain requirements. Place: a well-carpeted room in a hotel. Time: nighttime, blue moon, music somewhere between sexy and sacred like the Archangel Gabriel playing the sax. I would be taller, thinner, and more elegant, my lover a cross between Victor Manuel and Clint Eastwood, everything in slow motion as if we were floating on air. He would be skilled and knowledgeable, I ductile and weightless.

K's tongue moved laboriously inside my mouth, bumping into mine. I tried to avoid it, discovering a rotary movement that I could sometimes reverse: to the left, to the right, the left, twice each way, and then without pattern at all. K understood this as a signal of pleasure. Then I remembered the way it was in movies, so I put my hands around his neck and stroked his hair, smooth and expertly cut by his father's barber. I was doing this quite well when suddenly, lost in my movements, I felt something between my legs and took fright. I hadn't planned to go that far and felt no desire to. I was bored, I wanted to go home and have lunch. But what could I do? Scream like some savage? Cry like a foolish girl? I tried to act in the most adult fashion that I could. It was hard and dry with pain that took some time to subside. I think I stopped breathing, out of shock, and K took my lack of breath for a very erotic sign. He put his hand behind my head and kissed me on the forehead, on the eyes. That was what I liked the best. I stretched and stood. Then I summed up: my first sexual relations had taken place while sitting on a garage shelf between two cans of blue metallic automobile paint and a yellow watering can. Now I could hear what my sister was playing upstairs: *Dancing Queen.* Merry-go-round music, I thought.

With my hand in K's—he seemed unable to let me go—I went to look at myself in the bathroom mirror. Nothing. I had the same face. My nose had not grown wider nor my eyes bigger, nor my lips any redder. So such important events did not leave any marks. I took mental note of that. A small stain was the only evidence of the crime.

I went into the living room where my sister was recording the song....*and when you get a chance...*I sat by her side, feeling light years away from her.

I tried to help her, to put my mind to something else, and I'd almost succeeded when K arrived with a tray holding lots of cookies and two bowls of ice cream. A gesture of atonement? I began to shred my cookies and heap them on top of the ice cream, the way I like to do. "Let me feed you." I felt sorry for him. He was happy and I was the cause, but he didn't know what to do, how to love me or make me happy. He felt protective, paternal, responsible for me. I was rational enough to understand that we had not gotten to this point only through his actions, but through that terrible mixture of carelessness and curiosity that has always typified me. Shouldn't we go now, I asked.

"No," my sister said. "We're getting a ride. K talked to his father, and they're going to send him the car."

"You've never seen me drive," added K. I heard the message in his tone: we're accomplices. We have a past intimacy in common. Then we were in the car, the two of us in front and my sister in back. "Listen to that, what a surprise." Led Zeppelin,...*and she's buying a stairway to heaven.*

What was K feeling? I imagine he thought we'd been married in the cathedral. He gave me little kisses at every red light, Stop, and

Yield, while he sang *you are buying a stairway to heaven.* I looked at the street, the other cars, the people outside. What had I done? My god, how right my parents were to keep me tied up. I was sinful and deviant. No, it wasn't like that.

I loved K. I liked him. I cried when we quarreled, and I enjoyed our nights on the porch with music and his stories of school pranks and arguments with his father. He was so sweet. But from now on nothing would be the same. And what if we broke up? What if he told his friends? I wouldn't tell even if I were tied to the stake.

Stay for supper, my mother invited him. No thanks. He didn't want to impose on us. But he sat down alongside me at the table. He cut my chicken from the bones, sliced my green banana into delicate slivers, and brushed the hair out of my eyes. I smiled tolerantly, which was all I could bring myself to do. K danced with my sister, told jokes, wrote "I love you" on sheets of paper which he threw from the porch. I prayed for night to come so he would go home and I could be alone with my head and my vagina.

Finally he decided to leave. "Come down with me for a minute." Why? "I want to give you something." I didn't want to. "Okay, I'll bring it up. Wait for me." I sat on the stairway landing thinking that the stairs were white, granite, with splashes of black. He came back with a beautiful bouquet of flowers in a vase: pink and white gladiolas, red roses, carnations, and lilies, tied in a bow the color of a blue moon—and with a card. I love flowers, but these made me sad. "Bye. Call me when you get up, so I don't wake you." I went inside with my trophy.

"And those flowers?" They're from K. "But why?" I don't know. "The anteater sent them," my father said. "They're pretty. Give me a kiss and sleep well." Thanks, papa, I replied.

My bed of yesterday and today, my pillow, my Mafalda poster, my teddy bear. Would they love me the same as before? And K? When his euphoria of initiation passed, what would things be like? Out of weakness and adolescent snobbery, I thought, I had ruined something beautiful and tender that could have been slow and sweet. Now it wouldn't be. On the bed next to me, far removed from it all, my sister was sleeping the rhythmic sleep of those whose conscience is clear. Maybe she was dreaming of the zoo and the anteater we never saw, the ice cream and ABBA, her sister's charming and obliging boyfriend. Probably she wanted one just like him.

I cried a lot. For the distance that separated us and made us different. For not being the person my parents thought I was. For having been false and feigned with K, who would remember me with much affection as his "first time." I cried because I had emerged from the pages of the Brothers Grimm and, not very happily, entered those of Henry Miller—and because I had lost the unique and unrepeatable opportunity to enjoy the most important event of my life, which had not been sublime, dreamy, diaphanous, or ethereal. Not even heartbreaking or violent. Nothing. It had been sadly gray and uncomfortable. I cried a lot, though I didn't cry myself to sleep. I cried a lot, and I was up very late.

Translated by Dick Cluster.

This Time Pay Attention
To What I'm Saying

Marilyn Bobes

1.

It is three o'clock in the morning and the phone is ringing and finally it wakes us up. At this ungodly hour, who could it be but Cary? I want to get out, she said, I have to get out of this house right now. She was crying and kept repeating herself and sounded really bad. I'm completely fed up with him.

Cary, calm down. What is it? Good god, are you still hooked up with the musician? Is that it? Cary, answer me. Is it the music guy? But she hung up.

If this had been the first time it happened, we'd have rushed to her side.

Even last Wednesday, when she called at midnight, we didn't think twice about it. But, when we got there, guess what greeted us? There was Cary, completely different from her phone call, calm, smiling.

Oscar had returned from a late night shift. Cary was fixing his dinner. So there we were like two fools in the doorway. We tried to make up some lame excuse for our unannounced visit—something on the order of we were leaving the movies and noticed the lights were on and decided to stop by.

Alberto didn't say a word about it all the way home. Only today, while we were eating breakfast, did he suggest what I didn't even want to think about. I don't know, no one can tell another person what to do or how to find happiness. But, if Cary leaves Oscar to go back to Fausto, it would be suicidal. She'd have to be really crazy. She'd be trading something really valuable, something that could last, for a quagmire of hopeless dreams.

OK, so now I've told her. Cary, be careful what you do. The musician will never be good for you. There's always a point on the road to perdition when it's too late to turn back.

2.

It's really silly for him to try out a sporty look, and check himself out in the mirror after spending the whole morning seeing his reflection in the eyes of the female patients whose teeth he's pulling. He's a nice guy, who's really dedicated to his work, who would never fail to keep a date he has made, but of course he'll never give any of them his phone number—he's really careful about that—because they are the wives of other men. They have no right to bother us at home, he says, especially not when I am so wary of things that could threaten our relationship, and plunge us into chaos. That's what he told me yesterday, when Evita called him to say that she still didn't have her period. She tells him about her sex life with a breeziness that surprises me. It's almost as if she wanted to get revenge for something, it seems to me. I tell Oscar what I think, but he just attributes that type of conjecture to my pathological jealousy and says that it is perfectly normal for mature, civilized people to maintain some degree of intimacy even after they have separated.

I realized right away, when he told her let's talk about that later, that they were referring to me. I'm sure he told her that I refused to try on the earrings she bought. I mean she's pretty, but I'm much more so, and she shouldn't be so careless about her appearance, even if she's trying to seem intellectual. "Seem" is the operative word, which I'm sure he told her, along with my concern about the study with the light coming in from the left or the right —I can't really say for sure. Anyway, don't they realize that I can't write so much as an epigram in a room still filled with boxes of her tacky shoes—and photographs of her honeymoon. Was it Baconao they went to, that place near Santiago? I don't know.

Can't they understand that I detest all of it? And if it seems like posturing on my part, well just look at her. She refused to get married in a church so she could keep her standing as a militant, but she wore a fancy dress and veil that made her look like a big puff of cotton candy, given how fat she is and those boobs.

I ask myself why they got divorced since they are alike in so many ways. They both save money for vacations as if only those who go on vacation had a right to be wasteful. And the worst part is that every month he makes me give him thirty pesos, which I'd rather spend going out to a restaurant once in a while. But no, no restaurants for him because he loves spaghetti and we always have to fix it the same way with tomato sauce and cream cheese. Yuck. It's so boring, I can hardly stand it.

Of course, in this house I can be more relaxed. I'm freed from the telephone and from my mother's tears and I've distanced myself from the road to perdition.

The road to perdition.

We never stop to think about set phrases, but for some time now I've been asking myself where that road begins and what gets lost on the way to perdition--maybe even oneself. But, how can you know who you really are when the only thing you get to do is what others let you do—what other people propose, approve, and sanction as being correct?

When I tried to talk to Oscar about this, he just looked at me as if I were crazy.

I know that at times he thinks I am crazy, and I almost have gotten to the point of believing that I do have a screw loose, because it makes no sense to live someplace where the few times you go out you have to close all the windows and shut the doors to the terrace, just in case it rains and the mattresses and the pictures on the walls might get wet. And the pictures are only there because he read about the painters in some magazine. And he even takes me to art shows and looks at the oil paintings from a distance like someone making an effort to really, really understand, without even beginning to understand the reasons for his own obstinacy, without understanding, good heavens, that the real road to perdition is an attempt to understand.

To try to understand why he puts on that blue workman's outfit and then goes to run at the university stadium, to try to figure out why he should imagine that I might be jealous. I mean, really. Jealous of him? I scarcely find him attractive and I'm bored with his way of making love. His idea of passion is to try out an expression for the imaginary camera that is filming us and to repeat supposedly poetic words for the script he has prepared to sleep with a writer. Good lord—a writer who has spent her life trying to be treated like any other woman.

But it's really a lie. I don't want to be like other women. I don't want to be Evita, who avoids breaking in when men speak without even realizing what men say about us. Things like the Pablo Neruda line—supposedly romantic—that "I like you when you're silent because you seem almost absent." I could use that very line about many men, Oscar among them.

Of course he is a really good dentist. Alina told me so. And I know for sure that he truly likes to get people to open their mouths so that he can get rid of their cavities. But the bad part is that he doesn't actually get rid of them. He discovers them and fills them which is only an illusion of dental health, because when the filling falls out the teeth hurt more than ever and I should know because I've lost three.

That's why we eat spaghetti. So our fillings will not fall out, as if the world would be a cleaner, purer place for our having done so..

Every night before going to bed we make sure to brush our

teeth.

3.

To tell the truth, I still don't know how they managed. One day they showed up at my house to ask for a loan of twenty pesos. They had spent everything they had over the weekend.

They enjoyed that kind of madness. They would take a bus from the terminal and go off to Varadero beach, Cienfuegos, Trinidad or some other city. They stayed in the most expensive hotels and spent everything, drinking, eating in restaurants, living as if they were millionaires. On only two salaries, Fausto's and Cary's.

She came to her job at the ministry with big bags under her eyes. She could barely stand up. And every few minutes she would be at the water fountain. All because of a hangover.

I think that at times they barely ate. The only thing never missing from the dingy garret where she lived with the musician were bottles of rum.

One day Lazarita told me that at three in the morning she had gone with Cary and a guy named Daniel to the coast and that Fausto was there playing the flute until dawn.

That was another of the musician's customs. Before Cary moved in with him, he used to wake up the neighborhood playing the flute right outside one window or another of her house. No consideration for others. They had to call the police.

Of course it must be said that he was a likeable sort. To have lived with so many women he must have been likeable. A comb and some soap and water would have done him a world of good. But apparently his habit of being somewhat careless about his personal appearance came from being abandoned as a child when his mother went to live with a man and brought him from Sancti Spiritus to Havana. She sent him to the National School of Art so he could study music.

Caridad was so crazy about Fausto that after the famous money borrowing episode, when I told her what I thought, she insulted me right to my face.

I suggested that it wasn't right for a man to squander his salary that way, and she said that it seemed worse for a man to invite a woman to dinner and then expect her to sleep with him. She added, and this really ticked me off, that many women who consider themselves married and respectable put up with more infidelity than a stag has horns just to be able to ride in a car and live in a decent apartment.

It was enough to make me sick. We didn't talk for a month. Then she called me. Like always, crying. She swore that the part about access to a car wasn't personal, that I would always be her friend and that she felt lost. Her family wouldn't let the musician in the house. And now he was gone for days at a time. Especially after he found out she was pregnant.

Because as it turns out, Cary was pregnant. Thank goodness it didn't take a lot to convince her to end it. Fausto had already done his part. At first he promised to think it over, but in the end he didn't want a child. Fortunately for Cary.

And I think that was the moment when she realized that he didn't love her at all. Because although Cary had never cared for children, when she found out she was about to have one she got excited about having a baby. Cary wanting a baby! And no marriage ceremony! And with that crazy drunk who might have given her a mongoloid or retarded child.

Poor Cary, after all you have to feel sorry for her. She had hopes that if she bore a child, Fausto would change, that he would stop drinking, and would turn into a responsible man.

4.

A rock concert is not the best thing to listen to during meals, and the Beatles are passé. Oscar thinks that he should record songs by Barbara Streisand and Maria Bethania because that was the kind of music preferred by the women he slept with before I appeared. They never challenged the household order established by Evita.

Eva left as well.

I should have paid more attention to what they said. It's a shame that all the women left him, since he's a good man. But if they all left, he must have a problem and everyone laughed, knowing that if a man always got left by women, the problem must be...

Fausto didn't get left because he was always the one who went first. I can close my eyes and picture him on his knees in front of the empty niches of the cathedral swearing eternal love for me. What wouldn't he be capable of doing in the days preceding a paycheck, as long as I would pay for his drinks. Alina says he is a jerk. "In my entire life I have never paid even half of a bus fare for a man." She says it with pride as if it were almost a badge of honor. She almost hits me when I tell her that what seems humiliating to me is for a woman to serve a man just so he would pay for everything, and in spite of all the ways I have changed since then, I still believe that.

It's true that I don't pay for anything for anybody anymore, but if I don't it's because I don't want to be considered a pushover.

Alina says that's how men treat women who pay for things, like pushovers.

And there can be no doubt—both she and my mother are convinced of it—that Oscar is THE man because even though now we never go anywhere, when we did go out, he was the one who paid. They introduced him to me so that I wouldn't have to stay away from work with my stomach tied in knots and a splitting headache.

He's mild-mannered and calm and dresses with care and shaves, so different from Fausto.

Right away he took me dancing.

"But I don't know how to dance."

"That's fine because I don't like women who dance."

"But typically women like to dance and real men don't dance." And then I understood that I'd put my foot in my mouth because his face became flushed.

"That's the title of a novel, *Real Men Don't Dance,*" I said trying to recover, and then he showed me a perfect smile—the kind you only see in movies—and I discovered that his eyes were a strange yellow color.

"You're a girl who reads."

A girl who reads, Good Lord. I don't know why, but I felt like someone had poured cold water on me or kicked me.

"Yes, I'm a girl who reads."

I remember that I repeated it trying to take it in. It was said in an off-hand way, as if a girl who reads was nothing out of the ordinary.

5.

I accompanied her to the hospital. I will never forget her face when she came out of the anesthesia. She put her hands down on her stomach as if they had taken out her ovaries. I couldn't believe it. She began to cry.

Fausto, that hypocrite, was waiting for us outside with a bouquet of flowers. Cary took the flowers without even glancing at him. She had a detached look that expressed displeasure yet didn't seem impolite. She had a way of doing that.

And Fausto got the message. He understood fully once we were in the car and she asked Alberto to take her to her house in Miramar. She was withdrawn, remote, and didn't say a word the whole time. The musician didn't know how to act. He tried to make some jokes but nobody laughed. Then, obviously feeling awkward, he decided to get out at the first corner.

This time none of his concerts in front of Cary's house got him anywhere nor did his umpteen phone calls.

I'm tired of being mistreated, she confessed to me sometime later.

That seemed to be the ideal moment to get her to listen to reason. Oscar had just gotten divorced. I immediately thought of him. Why not? Like the Walt Disney movie with the roles reversed: the lord and his "lady" tramp. The crazy musician had turned Cary into a tramp. He brought out her worst qualities. The crazy part of her that, left unchecked, could overwhelm the good qualities. Just like the film about the doctor who invented a drug that turned him into a monster. The musician and his alcohol were a poison for Cary. The worst thing she ever did was meet him and fall in love with him. And that's taking into account all the lowlifes she'd met up with previously and all the entanglements that her dreamy illusions and stupidity had gotten her into.

6.

He must have some problem and now it seems to me that even that problem might have been less trifling than the obligation of putting up with him.

Put up with him but I'm not even sure what I mean by put up with because what is so terrible that I have to put up with. Oscar doesn't drink, he gets home on time, his contacts with other women are limited to quick exchanges of smiles and glances and the inoffensive weekly calls from Eva.

Alina says that what's happened is that I'm feeling nostalgia for Fausto and that is a feeling that I can't allow myself to have. I have to remember the tears I shed and how I made my mother cry. Resign myself to the fact that the relationship with Oscar is the only one that can restrain the tendency to get off track that I have had since I was young and that I have tried to curb in various ways.

The good thing is that I have friends and family and during my lifetime I've met up with a lot of really nice guys. The first was Alejandro.

It's curious but just now I realize that Alejandro also wanted to be a dentist and used the argument about the cavities to keep me from smoking. But in reality what bothered him was the tobacco smell. It's a disagreeable smell, men say, as if I, too, weren't bothered by unpleasant smells, like those of dental amalgams and ether.

Of course it's all happening because I'm not normal. Who could be bothered by such an aseptic smell? Yet it bothers me as much as I like the smell of aged rum. A good shot of rum while Fausto was playing records, putting the needle carefully in place for each song. But I don't need to think about that. I should remember what it was like the following morning when I had to get up at seven to catch a bus and spent the whole day feeling so miserable that I couldn't concentrate and could barely think.

Two times I called in sick to work, when the only sickness was a hangover. My fellow workers noticed and Alina herself, who at the time knew nothing about my life, recommended a checkup. It could be your gall bladder, although Lazarita thinks it's nerves or perhaps you're pregnant which isn't possible if you're not with someone. But hey, what you need is a man and then you'll see how this foolishness of being sick all the time will vanish.

7.

In spite of all the efforts I make to put myself in your place, I can only come up with one explanation: you're sick.

Yesterday you spent the afternoon with me, and when you walked out the door you seemed completely convinced that Oscar was the ideal man, the one you've been looking for your entire life; someone with whom to start a family and make a home.

I was relieved, confident that this time my arguments were not in vain and that the words I had employed to banish from your mind all those doubts and bad thoughts had not gone down the drain.

And then, all of a sudden, the phone call.

Perhaps Alberto is right and you need a psychiatrist right away. Someone to help you get out of the fantasy world you've been living in and get your feet on the ground. Otherwise you'll just turn into a pushover. Or worse yet into an alcoholic, like that blessed musician: a depraved man who only aims to totally disrupt your life and exploit you.

And you're still capable of feeling sorry for him? You say that he is too sensitive and that's why he gets drunk. That jerk, too sensitive? That's the last straw.

Oh, Cary, Cary: sometimes you seem like a creature without scruples; other times like an ingenuous adolescent. You're acting more like a teenager than a grown woman.

If I introduced you to Oscar, it was because I felt that after three or four dates you would end up falling in love with each other. For sure. You'd make such a nice couple! And you need someone serious, a helpmate, some stability. Every woman needs that. Don't tell me no, because I don't want to hear it. This time pay attention to what I'm saying.

Translated by Anne Fountain.

It's A Good Thing

Marilyn Bobes

Cary is a strange case. She doesn't care what people think about her. And instead of going swimming or arranging her clothes, she gives details about her private life to everybody with a kind of childish, foolish innocence, as if everyone saw the world with the same naturalness that she does. As if this sincerity could somehow protect her from the calumnies that gossip can provoke.

With Art, "Artie," nonetheless she acted like a lady. Who would have imagined? Such a well-bred and well-educated guy. But that didn't really matter to Cary. When you asked her why the relationship failed, she said it was her fault. After all, a woman who's had three marriages and so many boyfriends must simply be immature and/or unstable. And Art, such a good man, the victim of that devourer of men, that lady vampire who could never be satisfied.

Art gave Cary many gifts. He dressed her from head to toe. It must be said that he got her to do something that no one else had been able to do: get her focused on her appearance. He taught her something fundamental: that a woman has to be a woman, but she also has to look like a woman. Cary has never looked as pretty or well-dressed as when she was with Art. And just look what happened. Everybody realized it except her.

At first I thought they just had a good friendship, the kind that rarely occurs between a man and a woman. Because men just know how to be friends with other men. They have buddies to converse with and to discuss serious problems. If by chance they allow a woman to join the group or invite her to share a bottle of rum—something that inevitably accompanies the long monologues by which each one tries to prove how great, macho, and lively he is—they do it to show off in front of her, with the secret hope of carrying away the league championship, the best "touching" average, the best score for copping a feel. And all under the guise of drunken camaraderie.

Art was not like that. He didn't have buddies. And he didn't get drunk. He was always with Cary: in the dining room at lunch time, saving a seat for her at meetings, and passing her comical notes at work. When persons susceptible to caricature joined the department, Art and Cary would give them funny names. They're the ones who gave Cabrera the nickname Marco Polo because he talked about his trips all the time—to the Parthenon and Florence, for example, or how the Chinese were different from the stereotype that we Cubans have of them. A bit of an insult to the people of lesser means in the Ministry. (Although Marco Polo never noticed it, Patricia, the black woman who did the cleaning, scrunched her face and looked utterly disgusted whenever he carried on about the various airlines and airports. Poor thing. The only flights she'll ever take in her entire life are the short ones between Boyeros and Guantánamo—when good weather lets them fly.)

When Cabrera, with all his bluster, left the Department and went back to his office on the tenth floor, Art began to imitate him with such success that people laughed till they cried. And Cary did her part. She took a cigar, moistened it at the water fountain so it would look just right, and placed it between Art's lips so he could complete the caricature to perfection. It was the combined efforts of Art and Cary that made the jokes based on Cabrera so good and allowed us to vent our frustration over his petulance. Two years ago, Marco Polo deserted on an Aeroflot stopover in Gander, not even venturing to land in Mongolia.

At the time that Art came to the Department and took up with Cary, Pepe was not yet on the scene. And I remember it well because it happened right during the episode with Frank, a two-bit actor with roaming hands. Of course, none of the macho types was willing to do what Art did: go right up to the big-mouthed harasser and threaten to pop him one if he didn't leave Cary alone. No blood was shed because vice-minister Palacio himself and two or three of the chauffeurs, who were waiting around for their next assignments, separated Art and the actor before fists could fly.

And what a coward the harasser turned out to be. When they held him back his whole body trembled and he didn't even struggle to get free, although he kept shouting "Let go of me you bastards, let go, show some respect for a man," and a bunch of other nonsense all designed for show and bluster. Art, on the other hand, was willing to fight even though he looked pretty weak, with his wire rimmed glasses and a smallish chest that looked pitiful when compared to Frank's musculature.

After that incident, Cary began to really like Art and pay more attention to him. She even accepted his invitation to the ballet. It was on one of those Sundays when Pepe went to stay with the woman from the country and her little girl in the Casino Deportivo neighborhood. From there he couldn't even call Cary by phone because Briseida could be really fierce, and when he was with her he was cowed even though he managed to keep her fooled from week to week.

Art was one of those ballet fans who never misses a single performance and knows the choreography by heart, and can tell you which ballerina has done the most *fouettés* and which one has the best extension. That would be Amparito Brito, although Loipa, in her best moments was every bit as good as Amparo. And of course you still have to watch out for Loipa with her swan-like neck and almost perfect figure.

Those were the kinds of conversations he liked to have with Cary after they left the theatre and went to have something innocuous like *caña santa* at a place near the García Lorca theatre. That's where he first recited the famous verses by Baudelaire: *sois muette, sois sombre et plonge toute entière au gouffre de l'Ennui.* I remember because later that became a kind of pact between them.

And along with poetry, Art gave her a Good Morning greeting every day as she placed her purse on top of the desk. She dressed in purple, which according to Art was the color of sadness, of her sadness, the color most suited to the personality he determined to invent for her from the very moment he fell in love with her.

I really believe that Art, in spite of his problem, was in love with Cary. Alberto laughed every time I tried to convince him of Art's love for Cary. And in the end he was right. Without even meeting him, what he knew about Art made him shake his head and look disgusted. And it was he, who had always considered Cary's loves and adventures as women's topics, who told me one day very seriously: Alina, tell Cary not to give up Pepe for that ridiculous guy. I don't have anything against him, but Art seems pretty odd. And, in truth, ever since Albert said that I began to look at Art differently. And every day I liked him less and less.

But O.K. What happened with Pepe, happened, and Cary didn't have anyone else. To some degree, Art got her through the crisis with his cheerfulness and compliments. He asked her out: to theatres, to cabarets, to parties; he was always correct, never pushy, saying goodnight to her at the door of her house even if then he had to take three buses to get back to San Agustín where he lived with his mother, a delightful woman whom Cary immediately liked immensely.

The afternoon Art asked Cary to marry him, they were in fact in San Agustín. He had taken her there so she could try on a skirt and jacket outfit that Art's mother had sewn for Cary, following instructions from her son. And if truth be told, Art had an eye for dressing Cary that surpassed that of any woman I know. That tailor-made suit was one of the most elegant and tasteful outfits anyone could imagine. It looked like a creation by Dior, or Paco Rabanne or some other famous designer. Pale grey, fitted, with an impeccable cut and a small slit at the back of the skirt. And it made Cary look fabulous. Nonetheless, it was a suit that established respect, that made men try to behave with decorum and approach with discretion. Their compliments were expressed in a cautious, almost reverential manner.

That was another thing Cary learned from Art and that I, in turn, learned from Cary. How to wear clothing. And not just about how to look appealing but how to look fashionable. Wearing too many accessories, skimpy slip-on shoes, and cheap earrings actually makes you look less respectable and even less sensual. If you wear earrings, you can't add buckles, plastic bracelets, rings or necklaces, because they leave an impression of jangling trinkets and the image of a rather tacky woman with cheap taste who is therefore cheap herself.

On the other hand, if you are uncouth and boorish, you can bathe three times a day and everyone will still take you for a slob. Looking unkempt shows a lack of consideration and makes people think of you as a slouch and not take you seriously.

Art laid down the law with Cary. Solid colors and no garish oranges or reds. Eye shadow always very discreet and one shade lighter than your blouse or dress; shoes: close-toed, no sandals, slippers or clogs with half your heel hanging out. Art made all these suggestions and she followed them during the four months that they were married, and even after the divorce.

Because after the divorce, Cary was never quite the same. She gave up her jeans and made her house a more pleasant place, full of paintings, plants, and tasteful items all of which, according to Art, created a restful atmosphere and a sense of comfort that let you leave your problems at the door and enjoy a private life of equilibrium. That kind of peace lets a person face the difficulties of the outside world with optimism and the assuring sensation that the rear guard is covered.

Now you see. *Nadie es perfecto.* Nobody's perfect. It seemed that Cary had found the ideal man. But this time all the comments appeared to be on target and they coincided with Cary's complaints. With considerable reticence Cary decided to tell me one day about Art's nocturnal indifference: by even the most generous estimate Art had only slept with Cary on three occasions in all the time they were together.

Art is odd, said Cristina. Art is too clean, insinuated Nélida, from personnel. Art has too many quirks, commented Lidia, who was secretary to Palacio, the economic vice minister. Art likes ballet a little too much, insisted Cristina, getting close to the truth. The problem with Art is he's a fag, declared Alberto.

And that was the truth. Poor Cary. A bore, a self-destructive type, an egotist, and now a fag.

Everyone was aware of the end and no one more than me. Because I really want the best for Cary. And a gay man, even if he teaches you how to dress and decorate your house, is no kind of husband for a real woman.

When all was said and done, Cary had lasted longer than many in her circumstances would have. On Art's recommendation she began exercising at the Beauty Institute, which helped her expend excess energy and fall into bed exhausted at night. Because poor Art was going through a bad time; these changes in weather give him asthma, and he's always got a cold and feels sick. That was at first. Then she began to blame herself: maybe she was too fat or her breasts were too small. If she spent another week with that cold turkey she'd end up frigid from the complexes. And, I believe, that that was one of the main reasons that she fell so hard for the musician.

The musician, Cary confessed to me, made her feel like the prettiest and most desirable woman in the world. Right from the day she first met him, on the beach, he transmitted that feeling to her. Perhaps it was because, unlike the others, who fell in love with her sweetness, her personality, and her intelligence, the flute player was attracted by her bikini and her hips. And Cary says that even though he wasn't indelicate or gross in any way, his way of looking at her made it clear why he was interested.

It's not easy to understand Cary when she says things like that.

Most women complain that men just think about sex. But apparently she likes it when men prioritize that way and look at her as a female. Probably the trauma with Art exacerbated that dark side, that need to feel like a femme fatale, a vamp. The proof is that she slept with the musician almost the first night they went out, and the experience must not have been bad and it must have affected her in a strange way that I never dared to ask about. And I wouldn't dare to ask now because the truth is that Cary doesn't talk much about her sex life and it's a good thing.

Translated by Anne Fountain.

Sandra

Sonia Bravo Utrera

My name is Sandra. Sandra has a certain erotic sense and flavor, at least that's what I think. I'm here just like I could be anywhere else: I've lost all notion of who I am and it doesn't bother
me a bit. I escaped from myself three years ago and although sometimes I regret it, in point of fact I'm happy. I couldn't take it any
more. I had grown past the roof, yes the roof, because when the
crisis got worse, I heard someone say that the Germans were
through with socialism and that the solid Berlin wall fell when the
roof crashed down around them. And I wonder: the roof, what
roof? My roof was six feet high in an attic less than ten feet wide
where on hot afternoons I hid in search of solitude. All I did was
read. I read and read, from Kafka to my Corín Tellado romances,
rented for one peso from the lady next door. My literature professor made me recite Kafka's *Metamorphosis* from memory, and I
realized that the transformation was happening to me not to
Gregor, the protagonist gripped by the terror of the absurd. Of
course I was and still am very focused and never breathed a word
to the teacher about Donald Duck cartoons or the mother-of-pearl

princess in Corín Tellado, I was afraid she would look mockingly at me from behind her old 1960's eyeglasses. Strangely, her name is Sandra, like mine, but she's from another generation. I don't think she agrees about the roof and the Germans and the Berlin wall, and if she did she wouldn't say. She belongs to the *tabula rasa* generation: *The history of Cuba begins on January 1, 1959. Before that, we had no culture, no development, no education–nothing. Just Americans, whorehouses and Marines–understand?* Like everyone else in this country bereft of Marines and whorehouses, she's afraid and only talks about important things, such as the eight o'clock nightly news with Manolo Ortega, who comes on the air now without his Hatuey beer, which, as the story went around campus, got filled one night with urine but he had to drink it anyway, savoring the foam, since Hatuey paid the bill and he didn't have the balls to say Shit! What a country, Sandra, what a country: economic progress and class struggle. I've always thought that no one believes in anything, and less so now that a salary equals ten dollars and a person can hardly act like a *homosapienserectus* on a breakfast of herbal tea. That's why I made my decision, period the end: at all times you do what you have to do. On hot afternoons I left the attic and went down to the Malecón to examine our Creole lady ambassadors to the United Nations and the way they dressed: today Italians, yesterday the French contingent, tomorrow the Spaniards, and the day after that, the night will be evenly divided between the Germans and the Canadians and everyone will be happy. My mother says I've lost my mind, that she never saw such things in her own house, better to hit the books and go to college, which she could never do because her mother was from the countryside and had to feed her and three other kids, and my mother, the eldest, who learned to wash and iron like an expert, became literate with the Revolution and then worked as a cook and cleaning lady in Miramar—twenty diplomas as best worker, one for each of the twenty years of my life. She named me Sandra because she thought it sounded like mango and papaya, which are Cuban fruits, not California apples that come with the worm-infested dollar inside and, though she denies it, because Sandra was the heroine's name in *Together for Eternity*, the first romance novel she ever read in loose, wet pages from a Vanidades magazine she found in the basement of the subsidized student house where she worked, that she read over and over until she fell asleep from exhaustion during the long nights of Havana socialism. My father, whom I never knew, had his socialism, too, of an international stripe, and who knows where he's buried. He was a bodyguard for one of the commanders and came down from the Sierra with him and went with him to wage war in other places, leaving my mother and me here twenty years ago when no one expected anything to happen to the roof or the wall. A few months more and I could have been in college, with any luck studying philology and rereading Kafka, weaving Penelope into Ulysses, and I might have seriously begun analyzing literary visions from antiquity to the present time. But my visions, those that belong to me, defined the rules of this game. I started out staring at the Malecón, at the cars in front of the Riviera hotel, and then they stared back at me and I was being taken seriously by the United Nations: Italians, Spaniards, Germans, Canadians—plenty to choose from. With the Italians I would talk about Dante and the *Divina Comedia* while we made love, with the Spaniards about the chorizo my mother saw once in a blue moon in her poor childhood, that I had never even seen or tasted; with the Germans—well, what else? the roof and the wall. I'm an educated and politicized girl, so with the Canadians I have to be creative since to tell the truth I don't know much about them; no one ever talked about them in school. I imagined that one of them would discover in me an exotic princess who tasted of mango and papaya and after exploring my body in a foreign and universal tongue would propose to me, and period the end. No more revolution, no more attic, no college, no lit professor, no mother with lost dreams. Now it was my turn to dream and that's how my future was decided; rather than become a Kafkaesque insect to protest an unfair society I became a *puuuuta*, but of course I did it as an act of genuine protest. Hipólito, from Valencia, who was setting up some business in the new Cuba, exclaimed "Viva la clase obrera!" during his orgasms in my proletarian vagina; in two weeks with him I learned a lot about the history of Europe and the role the Europeans would play in preserving global balance, *of course the left must be cautious, but that doesn't mean reactionary, look at me with my modest capital I'm here to help Cuba because you know Sandra all the wealth is here on this side of the Atlantic,* he would say as he stated that Cuban women born of the proletariat tasted like fruit. In the end Hipólito brought the long-desired *chorizos* when he came to say goodbye and my mother cried disconsolately when he placed them on the kitchen table. He left one afternoon during a downpour and promised to call in a few days. I'm still waiting. However, I'm an optimist and consolation came in the form of Gianni, an Italian photographer who got it into his head to take nude pictures of me just for him and no one else; from nude poses we graduated to positions in bed and from bed Gianni jumped like a Neopolitan house on fire when the police knocked on the door of the Hotel Nacional. He got charged with pornography and attempted rape of minors at the Playa del Este. I got off with a fine because after all I was an adult and the cops were much more interested in the case of the eight- and ten-year-old boys that Gianni photographed with their gentle Caribbean genitals floating in the breeze on a beach. Hans and Gert, on the other hand, finally cleared up my doubts about Berlin and the wall and appeared more than confident in German supremacy on every front; the Canadians have proven to be more than discreet, except that I get confused over whether they're from Montreal or Quebec and yes sir, I do make some mistakes about English and French and the Canadian identity. Jesus! In school I learned Russian, and who can I talk to now that no Russians are on the Malecón because they have no dollars, and English, too, but on my own, so I could read T.S. Eliot in my spare time as a young working class intellectual with a promising future and a mother who cooked, washed and ironed in the subsidized student housing when our Russian comrades were still on radio and TV, before they disappeared at a stroke of the Partycentralcommittee pen, as a philosopher working as a cab driver in free Havana said with great dialectic intelligence. Yes, all this in three years, from

1990 to 1993. Today, October 12, 1993, in the lobby of the Capri hotel where Iím sitting, I dream about those stormy afternoons in the attic with Kafka and Eliot and go nuts thinking about how to tell them about this, my metamorphosis, painful and irreversible like Gregor's, rock-like and marble-smooth like Eliot's rhythms, and thoroughly irreversible because *nowaynowaynowayJosé*.

The other Sandra, my literature professor, saw me yesterday and smiled complicitly. I think she understands the reasons for my transformation and approves, she'd even be able to explain it, like performing an autopsy on a corpse, unemotionally, as one of the undesirable but feasible consequences of the socialist crisis in Cuba. I insist that I, the other Sandra with the turned-out legs in search of dollars, whose name was bestowed by my mother and the commander of the subsidized student house next door, the name in which two identical vowels dance with four consonants that explode in fricative sibilance; I, Sandra, whose name is reminiscent of mango and papaya; I, Sandra, daughter of the commander next door and my poor mother bearing up under the weight of destiny; I, Sandra, the un-disadvantaged student who might have been in college today; I, Sandra salamander, with the crocodile gullet and the snail-like waist, will find on this island in due time the mother-of-pearl prince from Tellado's tales, and it will happen here, under this sky and this sea, with its warm and pleasurable waves breaking on the shore of the city now lost but always found by its absent children, which is why I'm sitting here, waiting— Sorry, I can't go on about my life, a bunch of Japanese tourists are coming this way and now I know what haiku is. Go ahead and try, dear comfortable reader, to fit *sandrasalamandra* into any image worthy of a good haiku.

Translated by Nancy Festinger.

Decision

Sonia Bravo Utrera

I've decided to show my belly button, the time is right, why wait, fifty well-lived years under the belt now, I'd have to diet of course, it's a good time to diet now with mad cows cowering all over Europe, good time for broiled fish and chicken, delicious, you bet it's delicious, flatten this tummy and show my belly button that connects me to the whole world and not just my mother, what a great idea, who had time for such things in Cuba what with military training, voluntary labor, meetings with the Personnel Director, looking after the kids, what with all the shortages and slogans, life passed by and who noticed, yes ma'am, take the leap, the kids are grown now, Fernando won't object but that Rogelio will blow a fuse, he's old-fashioned like his father, an ancient bear-brain who thinks that women can get an education but it's better if they don't, and absolutely no belly buttons, he hit the roof when you let it drop at lunch last Sunday, see how well-fed and rested you are since you moved to Spain, when you told them that to carry out your complete and absolute liberation it wasn't enough to change boyfriends twice a year, you were compelled to bare your belly button like those cute Canary Island girls who get on the bus in their tight pants, sighing sigh after sigh, their pants no longer a fashion statement but surrogate jail guards, imprisoning the regrets of old and young men who know they'll have to settle for an eyeful of cute belly buttons, watch your hands, no touching, yes ma'am, take the leap, because Rogelio's girlfriend can't hold a candle to you with her slanting dashing eyes, yes they're dashing, she's Korean and speaks Canary dialect and Rogelio is so gaga over her now that he's starting to lose his identity now and doesn't know if he's Cuban or Canary or Korean, and Fer will be tickled, all he cares about is soccer and school, so what fun to have a mother who's fifty and looks forty, even more fun when her boyfriends enjoy soccer as much as they enjoy her; a belly button is personal property and if Sandra wants to show hers, let her, she had to put up with Dad didn't she, who told her that working women have to be home to wait on their husbands at night, and skirts are better than jeans, and sure, wear loose pants when you volunteer so they don't crowd your crotch because your crotch belongs to Daddy and you need it to give a giddyap to the kids, home by six in bed by ten, volunteer work does wonders for the spirit and target practice helps your aim, you're freer now than ever before, because Fernando and Rogelio are going to college and you were doing fine as an accounting assistant; once in a while you can watch a Brazilian soap opera but don't go thinking you're Doña Bella who wiggled her ass and her fruitcake to teach men all the pleasures of body and mind, that was a lie, a fantasy, you're Sandra and will always be Sandra, poor Dad who died in Nicaragua without a clue that you, dear Mom, would find consolation in your own belly button, sure, go ahead with the diet, fish and chicken take years off your life if you eat them with vegetables, you wasted enough time Sandra for this chance at absolute liberation, you'll put on sunscreen and go to the beach every weekend, you'll insert yourself into the tightest stretch jeans you can find, what do you care if the Korean girl narrows her eyes even more so she doesn't have to look and if Rogelio's cheeks turn red like a ripened tomato, Fernando always went along, he'll take you to a game with your belly button on parade and laugh at the shy ones, your desires are normal, you're only owning up to your humanity with the belly button that your parents gave you and that the midwife created, you're asserting your personality at age fifty, you're a newly discovered Hollywood star in the firmament of the Canary Islands, and anyway why the hell should she care about your belly button in the breeze, the lady whose house you clean, she never asked your age but did ask all about your past, that life you had in which sharing your belly button was not a possibility, so yes, go ahead, do it, Lola next door knows some great diets, on free days you can eat nuts and chicken broth with onions, you'll buy raisins to keep the energy going, you'll go to the Canteras beach on Saturday and Sunday, you'll lean on Fernando and his friends, they're all quick to laugh and easy-going like the sun, the sun is out today, today when you made a major decision, you forgive your children's father, may he rest in peace, you forgive him because he was a tough customer, fought against the contras but died for nothing and didn't see the beginning of the end for the Sandinistas, a rolling stone gathers no moss, you figured out a way to raise the boys and send them to college, Rogelio's a good dentist and Fernando a fine engineer, and the three of you found work in Las Palmas, before the Korean girl came on the scene, though first you had to go to the Spanish embassy and declare your father's Andalusian ancestors, and then you made tracks, landing in Madrid on December 31 five years ago, cleaning apartments in the cold and snow and babysitting while the boys were out working construction, and with your savings after two years you went to the Canary Islands because that's where Eladio lived, Eladio, the first boyfriend who ever suggested that your face was pretty and so was your belly button, and now Martin, the second boyfriend, who doesn't stand in your way and is amazed by your energy in the kitchen and in bed, he loves the idea of making your belly button the communal property of humanity but for Martin's exclusive use and enjoyment, yes ma'am, you're old enough to know what you want, go for it, now's the time, no sight more beautiful than your belly button on parade in the streets of Las Palmas, your youth is returning, Sandra, because what with guns going off, diapers, assets and obligations, your mother's death first and then your father's, and then the news that your husband disappeared, and the endless days thinking of how to fill your children's bellies, never, ever, ever did you have time to devote to your belly button.

Translated by Nancy Festinger.

The Authors & Translators

THE AUTHORS

NANCY ALONSO is a physiology professor in Havana. Her first book of stories, *Tirar la primera piedra [Throw the First Stone]*, won honorable mention in the annual contest of the Cuban National Union of Writers and Artists in 1995. She won the 2002 Alba de Céspedes award for her second book of stories, *Cerrado por reformas [Closed for Repairs]*, published in 2003 .

AIDA BAHR has recently completed a novel, *Las voces y los ecos [Voices and Echoes]*, and is at work on another one. She is director of a publishing house in Santiago, Cuba, Ediciones Oriente, and editor of their magazine. Her work has appeared in many anthologies in Spanish and in translation into other languages. She is the author of several collections of stories, including *Hay un gato en la ventana [There's a Cat in the Window]* (1984), *Ellas de noche [Women at Night]* (1989), *Espejismos [Mirror Images]* (1998), and several screenplays.

MARILYN BOBES is a short story writer, poet and journalist who was born in Havana. She studied history at the University of Havana, and worked a a journalist for the Latin American press agency, Prensa Latina, and for the magazine *Revolución y Cultura*. In 1979 she received the David Award for Poetry for her book *La aguja en el pajar [Needle in the Haystack]*. For her fiction, she has received an Edmundo Valdés award (Mexico, 1993) and second place in the Magda Portal competition (Peru, 1994). Her books include *Hallar el modo* (poetry, 1989), and *Alguien tiene que llorar [Somebody Has to Cry]*, (from which the stories included here are taken) winner of the Casa de las Americas prize in 1995, and *Alguien tiene que llorar otra vez* (2001). She was a co-editor of the anthology of Cuban women's stories *Estatuas de sal [Pillars of Salt]*(1996).

SONIA BRAVO UTRERA holds a Ph.D. in philology and is a university professor, translator and writer, currently teaching at the

University de Las Palmas de Gran Canaria, Spain. She writes short stories, poetry, and literary criticism. Her current focus is on the Cuban exile experience from an ironic and unprejudiced point of view. She has translated early British travel accounts of the Canary Islands, Russian poetry and narrative, as well as prose and poetry from the Vienna school. Her translations and articles on diverse literary subjects have been published in Argentina, Uruguay, Spain, Cuba, Mexico and Russia. She is currently translating Robert Frost and analyzing translations of his work into Spanish.

Cuban feminist scholar LUISA CAMPUZANO is a founder (in 1994) and director of the Women's Studies program at Casa de las Américas in Havana, She was a professor of literature at the University of Habana before she retired in 2000. Her distinguished list of publications on Latin American culture and history includes over seventy articles and a dozen books, including a recent study of magical realist Alejo Carpentier, *Carpentier entonces y ahora* (1997) and the four-volume edited collection, *Mujeres latinoamericanas: siglos XVI al XX [Latin American Women, 16th to 20th Centuries]*.

ADELAIDA FERNÁNDEZ DE JUAN is a physician specializing in internal medicine, and author of many short stories, including those published in the volume *Dolly y otros cuentos africanos* (1994) about her experiences in Zambia 1988-90. It appeared in English as *Dolly and Other African Tales*. Her second story collection, *Oh vida [Oh Life]* (1998) won the National Short Story Prize of the Cuban National Union of Writers and Artists.

MYLENE FERNÁNDEZ PINTADO is a practicing lawyer who represents the Instituto Cubano del Arte e Industria Cinematográficos (ICAIC). Her stories have won prizes in the La Gaceta de Cuba competitions, in the Spanish 1998 III Premio de NH de Relatos awards, and the Cuban National Union of Writers and Artists' Premio David in Cuba, for her collection of short stories,

Anhedonia (1999). Her novel *El otro lado del espejo* [*The Other Side of the Mirror*] has just been published. She also authored several volumes of short stories. Her work has appeared in many anthologies in Spanish and in translation.

ENA LUCÍA PORTELA, born in Havana where she still lives, is a novelist and short story writer. She won the UNEAC National Novel Prize in 1997 for her first novel *El pájaro: tinta china y pincel* [*The Bird: Chinese Ink and Pen*], published in 1999, as was her collection of short stories, *Una extraña entre las piedras* [*A Strange Woman Among the Stones*]. She was the recipient of the Juan Rulfo Short Story Prize given by Radio France International in 1999 for her short story, "El viejo, el asesino y yo" ["The Old Man, the Assassin and I"]. Her novel *La sombra del caminante* [*The Walker's Shadow*] was published in 2001, and a third novel, *Cien botellas en una pared* [*One Hundred Bottles on a Wall*], won the Jaen Novel Prize in Spain in 2002.

KARLA SUAREZ was born in Havana, and presently resides in Paris, where she is a systems engineer, much of the year. Her collection of stories, *Espuma* [*Foam*], published in 1999, which includes the stories included here, has won many awards. A second collection of stories, *Carroza para actores* [*Stagecoach for Actors*] appeared in 2001. Her first novel, *Silencios* [*Silences*], received the Lengua de Trapo Fiction Prize in 1999, and has been translated into many languages.

ANNA LIDIA VEGA SEROVA was born in St. Petersburg, Russia, daughter of a Cuban father and a Russian mother. She has lived in Havana since she was twenty and writes exclusively in Spanish. She won the 1996 Special Prize of the Asociación Hermanos Saíz, and the 1997 Premio David for her collection of stories *Bad Painting* (1997). Her second volume of stories, *Catálogo de mascotas* [*Catalog of Mascots*} was published in 1998, and the third, *Limpiando ventanas y espejos* [*Cleaning Windows and Mirrors*] in 2001. A novel, *Noche de ronda* [*Nightwatch*] was published in 2002.

MIRTA YAÑEZ has written fiction, poetry, literary criticism, and children's books and has taught Latin American literature at the University of Havana. In 1988 and '90 she won the Critics' Prize for the story collection *El Diablo son las cosas* [*What the Devil*] and for the essay "La narrativa del romanticismo en Latinoamérica" ["Romantic Narrative in Latin America"]. Other books she has published include *Las visitas y otros poemas* [*The Visits and Other Poems*] (1986) and *Una memoria de elefante* [*An Elephant's Memory*] (1991). She is the co-editor of the anthology of Cuban women's stories *Estatuas de sal* [*Pillars of Salt*] published in 1996, and the editor of *Cubana: Contemporary Fiction by Cuban Women* (1998).

THE TRANSLATORS

MARY G. BERG's recent translations from Spanish include novels: *I've Forgotten Your Name* (forthcoming) by Martha Rivera (Dominican Republic); *River of Sorrows* (2000) by Libertad Demitrópulos (Argentina); and *Ximena at the Crossroads* (1998) by Laura Riesco (Peru), as well as stories, women's travel accounts, literary criticism, and collections of poetry, most recently poems by Carlota Caulfield and *Starry Night* (1996) by Marjorie Agosín (Chile). She teaches at Harvard Extension and is a Scholar at the Women's Studies Research Center at Brandeis University, where she writes about Latin American writers, including Clorinda Matto de Turner, Juana Manuela Gorriti, Soledad Acosta de Samper, and contemporary Cubans.

PAMELA CARMELL teaches Spanish in St. Louis. She is a founding member of the St. Louis Translators Roundtable. She has translated Luisa Valenzuela, Ena Lucía Portela, Mirta Yáñez, and Carlos Cortés among others. Her translations have appeared in numerous magazines and anthologies. Her translation of Antonio Larreta's novel, *The Last Portrait of the Duchess of Alba* was a Book of the Month Club selection. Her translation of poems by Belkis Cuza Male, *Woman on the Front Lines*, received the Witter Bynner Prize.

Her translations of poems by Nancy Morejón will be included in a collection to be published by White Pine Press.

DICK CLUSTER's translations of Cuban fiction include *Cubana: Contemporary Ficton by Cuban Women* (Beacon, 1998, ed. Mirta Yáñez, tr., with Cindy Schuster); Pedro de Jesús, *Frigid Tales* (City Lights, 2002); Alejandro Hernández Diaz, *The Cuban Mile* (Latin American Literary Review Press, 1998); Antonio José Ponte, *In the Cold of the Malecón and Other Stories* (City Lights, 2000); Leonardo Padura, *Mascaras* (selection, Whereabouts Press, 2002); and Abel Prieto, *The Flight of the Cat* (forthcoming). He is also the author of the novels *Return to Sender* (Dutton, 1988), *Repulse Monkey* (Dutton, 1989), and *Obligations of the Bone* (St. Martins, 1992), and translator of Cuban political scientist Rafael Hernández's essay collection *Looking at Cuba* (University Press of Florida, 2003).

SARA E. COOPER is currently an Assistant Professor of Spanish and Women's Studies at California State University, Chico. She has published articles on Alejo Carpentier, Alma López and Cherríe Moraga, Marilene Felinto, and Cristina Peri Rossi. Two of her translations were included in *Urban Voices: Contemporary Short Stories From Brazil*. Current projects include a critical analysis of queer family and women in Latin American literature and the editing of two volumes: a multi-authored volume of critical essays on family systems in Hispanic literature and a collection of translated short stories by the Cuban writer Mirta Yáñez.

CRISTINA DE LA TORRE has translated three novels: *Absent Love (Crónica del desamor)* by Rosa Montero (Spain, translated in collaboration with Diana Glad), *Mirror Images (Joc de miralls/Por persona interpuesta)* by Carmen Riera (Spain) and *A Single, Numberless Death (Una sola muerte numerosa)* by Nora Strejilevich (Argentina) as well as numerous short stories, many of them by authors from Cuba where she was born. She lives in Atlanta and teaches Spanish at Emory University.

NANCY FESTINGER is a native New Yorker with published translations from French, Spanish and modern Provençal. She works as Chief Interpreter in the federal court in Manhattan and is editor of *Proteus*, the newsletter of the National Association of Judiciary Interpreters and Translators.

ANNE FOUNTAIN teaches Latin American literature and culture at San Jose State University. She has taught at the University of Southern Mississippi, the University of South Florida, and Peace College, where she was named Alumnae Distinguished Professor in 1994. She is the author of *Versos Sencillos by José Martí–A Translation* [Romance Monographs, 2000] and *José Martí and U.S. Writers* [University Press of Florida, 2003].

A Brief Selected Bibliography of Books
By and About Contemporary Cuban Women Writers:

Alonso, Nancy. *Tirar la primera piedra.* La Habana: Letras Cubanas, 1997.
  Cerrado por reformas. La Habana: Letras Cubanas, 2003.
Araújo, Nara. "A escritura da mudanca: novissimas narradoras cubanas," in
  Márcia Hoppe Navarro, ed., *Rompendo o silencio.* Porto Alegre:
  UFRGS, 1995.
Bahr, Aida. *Espejísmos.* La Habana: Unión, 1998
  Hay un gato en la ventana. 1984
  Ellas de noche. 1989.
Bobes, Marilyn. *Alguien tiene que llorar.* La Habana-Bogotá: Casa de las
  Américas/Colcultura,1995.
  Alguien tiene que llorar otra vez. La Habana: Unión, 2001
Cruz, Mary. *Niña Tula. La Habana:* Letras Cubanas, 1998.
  Colombo de Terrarrubra. La Habana: Unión, 1994.
  El que llora sangre. La Habana: Unión, 2001
  Tula. La Habana: Unión, 2001
Davies, Catherine. *A Place in the Sun? Women Writers in Twentieth-century Cuba.*
  London, New Jersey: Zed Books, 1997.
Díaz Llanillo, Esther. *Cuentos antes y después del sueño.* La Habana: Letras
  Cubanas, 1999.
Fernández de Juan, Adelaida. *Dolly y otros cuentos africanos.* La Habana: Letras
  Cubanas, 1994
  Dolly and Other Stories from Africa. Translated by Lucy Robinson,
  Esperanza Devesa and Zilpha Ellis. Toronto: Lugus Libros, 1995.
  Oh Vida. La Habana: Unión, 1999.
Fernández Pintado, Mylene. *Anhedonia.* La Habana: Unión 1999.
  Historias del otro. Santiago de Cuba, Ed. Oriente, 2000.
Fowler, Victor. *La maldición: una historia del placer como conquista.* La Habana:
  Letras Cubanas,1998.
Llana, María Elena. *Castillos de naipes.* La Habana: Unión, 1998.
  La reja. 1965
  Casas del Vedado. La Habana: Letras Cubanas, 1983.
Mateo, Margarita. *Ella escribía poscrítica.* La Habana: Ed. Abril, 1995.
Picart, Gina. *El druída.* La Habana: Ed.Extramuros, 2000.
Portela, Ena Lucia. *El pájaro: pincel y tinta china.* La Habana: Unión, 1999
  Una extraña entre las piedras. La Habana: Letras Cubanas, 1999.
  La sombra del caminante. La Habana: Unión, 2001
  Cien botellas en la pared. 2002
Redonet, Salvador, ed. *Los últimos serán los primeros.* La Habana: Letras
  Cubanas, 1993.

Rojas, Marta. *El columpio de Rey Spencer.* La Habana: Letras Cubanas, 1996
   Santa lujuría. La Habana: Letras Cubanas, 1998.
Sánchez Gallinal, Margarita. *Gloria Isla.* La Habana: Letras Cubanas, 2001.
Santos, Mercedes. *El monte de Venus.* La Habana: Letras Cubanas, 2001.
Suárez, Karla. *Espuma.* La Habana: Letras Cubanas, 1999.
   Silencios. Madrid: Ed. Lengua de Trapo, 1999.
   Carroza para actores. Bogot·: Ed. Norma, 2001.
Vega Serova, Anna Lidia. *Bad painting.* La Habana: Unión, 1998.
   Catálogo de mascotas. La Habana: Letras Cubanas, 1999.
   Limpiando ventanas y espejos. La Habana: Unión, 2001.
   Noche de ronda. Tenerife: Baile del Sol, 2002
Yáñez, Mirta. *Narraciones desordenadas e incompletas.* La Habana: Letras
   Cubanas, 1997.
   and Marilyn Bobes, ed. *Estatuas de sal. Cuentistas cubanas contem-
   poráneas.* La Habana: Unión, 1996.
   Selection in English, Mirta Yáñez, ed. *Cubana: Contemporary
   Fiction by Cuban Women.* Translated by Dick Cluster and Cindy
   Schuster. Boston: Beacon Press, 1998.

THE WHITE PINE PRESS SECRET WEAVERS SERIES
Series General Editor: Marjorie Agosín

Dedicated to bringing the rich and varied writing
by Latin American women to the English-speaking audience.

Volume 16
A WOMAN IN HER GARDEN
SELECTED POEMS OF DULCE MARÍA LOYNAZ
Translated by Judith Kerman
176 pages $16.00

Volume 15
GABRIELA MISTRAL: RECADOS ON WOMEN
Translated by Jacqueline C. Nanfito
224 pages $16.00

Volume 14
RIVER OF SORROWS
A Novel by Libertad Demitropulos
Translated by Mary G. Berg
160 pages $14.00

Volume 13
A SECRET WEAVERS ANTHOLOGY:
SELECTIONS FROM THE WHITE PINE PRESS SECRET WEAVERS SERIES
232 pages $14.00

Volume 12
XIMENA AT THE CROSSROADS
A novel by Laura Riesco
Translated by Mary G. Bert
240 pages $14.00

Volume 11
A NECKLACE OF WORDS
Short Fiction by Mexican Women
152 PAGES $14.00

Volume 10
THE LOST CHRONICLES OF TERRA FIRMA
A Novel by Rosario Aguilar
Translated by Edward Waters Hood
192 pages $13.00

Other Latin American Titles

Magical Sites: Women Travelers in 19th Century Latin America
Edited by Marjorie Agosín and Julie Leveson
256 PAGES $17.00

A Woman's Gaze: Latin American Women Artists
Edited by Marjorie Agosín
264 PAGES $20.00

An Absence of Shadows
Poems on Human Rights by Marjorie Agosín
212 pages $15.00

Windows That Open Inward:
POEMS BY PABLO NERUDA   PHOTOGRAPHS BY MILTON ROGOVIN
Translated by Bly, Maloney, Merwin, O'Daly, Reid, Vega, Wright
96 pages $20.00

Neruda at Isla Negra
POEMS BY PABLO NERUDA   PHOTOGRAPHS BY MILTON ROGOVIN
Translated by Jacketti, Maloney & Zlotchew
127 pages $15.00

Starry Night
Poems by Marjorie Agosín
Translated by Mary G. Berg
96 pages $12.00

Ashes of Revolt
Essays by Marjorie Agosín
128 pages $13.00

SARGASSO
Poems by Marjorie Agosín
Translated by Cola Franzen
92 pages $12.00   Bilingual

Light and Shadows
Poems by Juan Ramon Jimenez
Translated by Robert Bly, Dennis Maloney, Clark Zlotchew
70 pages $9.00